"Robert McBrearty's stories occupy a — where the daft becomes heartfelt, the dangerous becomes ordinary, and the ordinary becomes downright odd –and where the act of writing is appropriately worthy of awe. A world, in other words, seen through a pane of absurdist old glass. The stories in *Episode* are McBrearty at the top of his unique form: wry, arresting, and unshakeable."

-David Wroblewski,
author *The Story of Edgar Sawtelle*
Oprah's Book Club selection

"We think McBrearty's writing is especially noteworthy for its blend of humor and pathos, and brings to American fiction many of the same strengths of Sherwood Anderson's writing."

-Michael Spear,
Co-President of the Sherwood Anderson Foundation

"McBrearty finds those moments in life when we reveal ourselves--sometimes to our own surprise–and weaves around them tales of understanding and misunderstanding that reach deep into common human experience. The stories in *Episode* will stick to your ribs."

-Steven Wingate, author of *Wifeshoppping*, Winner of the 2007 Bakeless Prize from the Bread Loaf Writers' Conference

"McBrearty is one of those sneaky writers. Because his style is so enjoyable and his humor so instinctive, he puts us at ease from the opening line. We're sitting by a fire, catching up with old friends. But then comes the twist, the poignant reflection, that subversive hint of pathos. This doesn't mean we stop laughing or enjoying the company. It's just that we're thinking and feeling too, taking in something lasting and true, grateful to have placed our trust in a master storyteller."

-Tom LaMarr, author of *October Revolution* and
Hallelujah City

"With the grace and grittiness of a blue collar John Cheever, Robert McBrearty zeroes in on the American soul with a funny, redemptive wit. His stories are masterful explorations of the human condition that also instruct the heart in ways that are always surprising, always compassionate. After quietly publishing for many years in some of the most respected literary magazines in the country, McBrearty smacks a home run with this new collection and establishes himself as one of the finest short story writers around."

-Timothy Hillmer, Winner of the Colorado Book Award
and author of *Ravenhill*

From Reviews of McBrearty's previous collection,
A Night at the Y:

"What threads through McBrearty's warm and engaging collection is a humaneness toward his characters, and a gentle, sad irony that pervades their world views."

-Robin Hemley, *The Chicago Tribune*

"The modern-day Walter Mittys of these 12 humorous stories, McBrearty's debut, shuffle carefully from their humdrum existences into wider, more exhilarating, and often quite humorous worlds."

-Publisher's Weekly

Episode

Robert Garner McBrearty

Pocol Press
Clifton, VA

POCOL PRESS

Published in the United States of America
by Pocol Press
6023 Pocol Drive
Clifton VA 20124
www.pocolpress.com

Publisher's Cataloguing-in-Publication

McBrearty, Robert Garner, 1954-

Episode / Robert Garner McBrearty. – 1st ed. – Clifton, VA : Pocol Press, c2009.

p.; cm.

ISBN: 978-1-929763-42-9

1. Short stories, American. 2. American fiction. I. Title

PS3563.C33358 E65 2009
813.54--dc22   0903

Acknowledgments

My writer's journey has been graced by the love of family and the companionship of good writing friends along the way. I would like to thank my father, William, and my mother, Virginia, who typed my early manuscripts and changed some of the lines for the better, my sisters Mary Ella and Pamela, my younger brothers Kevin and Gerald, founding members of the Western Touring Society, and my eldest brother Steve, who has walked the writer's walk with me the longest, ever since we were teenagers. A special thanks, too, to the Metke family, Pat and Polly and Mike and Kathie and Mark, and to all my in-laws and nieces and nephews, all part of the story.

My path as a writer has been made immeasurably happier by the friendship of fellow writers, from various times and places, too many to mention at this time, but for now, I would like to thank: Jack Smith, who as the editor of Green Hills Literary Lantern first published several of these stories and who has provided ongoing support and friendship for many years. As well, I'd like to thank Barry Kitterman, Tom Lamarr Jones, Tim Hillmer, Karen Palmer, Dave Wroblewski and all my friends from the old Boulder writers' group, Steven Wingate, Sigman Byrd, Don Eron, Catherine Kunce and all my friends at the University of Colorado, Philip Brady, Robert Lunday, Mitzi Mabe, Don Thompson, Dick and Debbie Stein, David Kysilko, Chris Datta, and Jim Jamieson, who wrote stories beside me at the Bellas Artes way back in the San Miguel days. Thank you all. Your friendship has made all the difference.

Professional Acknowledgments

I am deeply grateful to the Sherwood Anderson Foundation for its 2007 Sherwood Anderson Foundation Fiction Award which provided generous financial help and a wonderful boost to the writing morale.

Stories from this collection first appeared in:
North American Review: "Dinsmore's Paradox"; "Episode."
  StoryQuarterly: "Excellence."
  Narrative: "Teach Us."
  Green Hills Literary Lantern: "The Comeback"; "Transformations"; "The Director."

The author also gratefully acknowledges Stories on Stage in Denver and the Texas Bound show at the Dallas Museum of Art for hosting dramatized readings of "The Comeback" and "In the Bar."

Dedication

For my beloved Mary Ellen, and for Zane and Ian,
ever my treasures

Table of Contents

Episode

My older brother Len's off his meds again. I've felt his breakdown coming the last couple of days, though my father hasn't wanted to face up to it yet. This morning Len came into my bedroom and looked at one of my paintings on the wall, something I'd done in art school, an abstract southwestern landscape sort of thing, and not all that great. He stared at it, riveted, his eyes tearing up. "That's the most beautiful painting I've ever seen," he said. "That should be in the Dallas Museum of Art. That should be in the Louvre." With his strong arms, he drew me to his chest. "I can *feel* that horse between my thighs. That's me with the lance in my hands." He moved closer to the painting, eyes round and shiny. "No, I'm both. I'm the Comanche *and* the one being chased. God, that's brilliant! You're a *genius!*" I stared at my painting, but hard as I tried I could not see a single Comanche. At least I had not consciously included an Indian in the painting. There was only the prairie rolling away to the distance, and some trees and boulders and lots of colorful swirls. He released me from his embrace, then gripped both my hands and held them gently in his calloused palms. "Don't do manual labor with these," he said. "Don't be like me. I'll send you money when you need it."

He disappeared for the day, and now he's surfaced late at night, and we sit at the kitchen table as he sips whiskey, a vain attempt to calm himself. Every few seconds, his hand opens and shuts like a man giving blood. Len's thirty-two, I'm twenty-five, but since he started having his bipolar disorder a few years ago, I feel like the older brother. He moved back home with my father a few months ago, and I'm back home this summer after grad school, trying to get my bearings and move on.

He squints his eyes, cocks an ear, listening for something, listening maybe for the sounds of the horses' hooves, the horses carrying the Comanches back through time into a moonlight raid on our house in the hilly suburbs north of Austin. Len had a thing about the Comanches, even when we were kids; in a kind of love and hate he'd talk in awe of them as the greatest horse warriors who ever lived. He's been staying up all night this week, reading Larry McMurtry's *Lonesome Dove* trilogy, James Michener's *Texas,* and my mother's roots material about our family's frontier days, devouring hundreds of pages of the novels and the family lore, apparently not the best reading material if you're manic.

I take a breath, trying to steady my voice when I speak. "Listen, Len," I say, "I talked to Dr. Wilson."

He lurches back as if stabbed, eyes widening at the mention of Dr. Wilson, the psychiatrist whom he's seen off and on for the last few years. "That old hack?" he says. "Doctor Electrode? You got anybody else on the list? I mean, Kenneth, *really...*" He leans in close, breathing his whisky breath in my face, eyes turning squinty and wizened, like a con man working a deal. "Do we have any back up? Do we have a fucking plan here or not?"

"I should drive you down to the hospital, Len. You know, just get checked out."

His voice edges into bitterness. "You mean checked *in?* Whose side are you on, Kenneth? Whose side?"

I feel my throat tightening. "I'm on your side, Len, you know that."

He takes another swig at his whiskey. "Hey, I'm feeling good. I can handle this. This will all be gone in the morning. We'll play golf. Do you want to play golf in the morning? Because I plan to play golf in the morning, and I'd like you to come." He smiles too widely. "It'll be great, playing golf with you again." He cackles with sudden laughter. "I'm not carrying your bag anymore! Remember the way you used to make me carry your bag when you got tired? You're old enough to carry your own damn bag this time!"

I sit there, not answering, until he demands, "So do you want to play golf or not?"

I shrug my shoulders. "Sure, Len, whatever."

He lets out a long breath between tight lips, and leans in, eyes anxious. "Seriously, do I seem a little weird or something?"

"Oh not, not at all. You don't seem weird at all, Len."

His shoulders shake with quiet laughter as he gets the sarcasm, knowing I think he's being weird as hell, but the opening allows me to tell him the truth. "Len, I think you're having an episode. We've got to get some help."

He lowers his head, contemplates the suggestion for a moment, considers the weeks ahead in the hospital, the medications that flatten him out, and he sits back, squaring his shoulders as if to ward off something coming at him too fast and hard. "It happened here," he says in a hushed voice. "Right here. Close your eyes. Listen."

I stare at him, until he hisses, *"Close your eyes."*

I close my eyes, and I hear a faint wind against the windows. I hear his breathing, heavy and agitated. I hear the tinkle of ice in his glass. *"Do you hear it?"* he asks. I keep my eyes closed. "Hear what, Len? Hear what?"

"The screaming."

I open my eyes. His lips tremble. "Do you get it now?" he asks. "It happened here, right here. Mother knew. She hinted at it. She was going to break it to me first. She knew I was the only one who could handle it."

"What are you talking about?"

"Her roots stuff she was always looking into. Great-great Uncle Ira, the one who fought the Comanches?"

"I don't remember anything about it."

"God, how could I have missed it? Can't you hear the screaming? People *died* here. That's what she was trying to tell me. The house is full of spirits. It always has been."

I shake my head, though I get a tingle in my spine. "I just hear the wind, Len. It's just the wind."

He smiles, nods his head with the pretend patience of one dealing with a slow-learning child. "Remember the arrowheads we found when we were kids?"

"Mom said those were from a peaceful tribe."

"Of course she would tell you that. She tried to protect you." He leans in close, eyes gouging into mine, his voice a rapid, hoarse whisper. "She *knew.* She referred to a ranch not far from here. A ranch where Uncle Ira lived with his wife and son. But it was *here.* Our house is built right over the bloody soil. *This* is where they fought and died." "In the *kitchen?*" I rock back in my chair, creating a little more space between us. "Holy shit, Len, you're freaking the hell out of me."

He stares at me, eyes glittering. "They killed his wife and made off with the little boy. He grew up with the Comanches, but he was ransomed back. Only he was never the same. He was wild. He could never adjust." Len's been hiding something in his lap and now he brings it up onto the table, a butcher knife from one of our kitchen drawers. "They were up in the hills watching. Then they rode in. It was pure adrenaline,

4

Kenneth. Late at night, listening, wondering if this was the night they'd punch your ticket. It's coming clear to me now. My God, it all makes sense now."

He presses the point of the knife against the Formica table and spins it. He clasps it during its wobbly rotation. "I like knives," he says. "Do you like knives?"

"They're okay," I say, hearing the quiver in my voice. "I kind of like butter knives. Do you want me to get you a butter knife?"

"I've always liked sharp knives," he says. "The beauty, the power, the symmetry." He tests the air with the blade. Short and thick-muscled, Len's a pretty tough guy from his years of construction work and studying the martial arts. He's let his hair get shaggy and his ragged beard has got some streaks of blood or ketchup in it. He stands and swoops around the kitchen, doing deep knee bends, coming up, sweeping the air with the knife. "Come at me," he whispers to an imaginary enemy.

We hear a cough in the hallway, a clearing of a throat, and Len's face suddenly changes. He retreats to his chair at the kitchen table, and as if some calming wax has been spread over his features, his wild eyes sink inward, his agitated brow seals into a smooth surface, and with a quick motion he hides the knife beneath his shirt.

"You boys are up late," my father says, wandering in his old bathrobe into the kitchen, going to the sink for a glass of water. Maybe my father's seen the knife, but he doesn't let on. I think he tells himself he hasn't seen it.

Since my mother's death a year ago, he wears an eternally fragile, bewildered expression. He sleeps poorly, in his tattered bathrobe moves about the house like a ghost, checking doors and windows in the night. Lately, for the first time I can remember, he seems

5

troubled by his Korean War experiences. He never talked about the war when we were growing up, and even now he says little, but sometimes he gets a far away look. A couple of mornings ago he stood at the sliding glass door, looking at our large, well-cared for backyard, and he said to himself, quite clearly and distinctly, continuing an interior conversation, "He's been dead all these years. He never had a chance."

I joined him at the glass door and asked him whom he was referring to. My father likes to be asked questions, and if he doesn't want to answer, he'll just avoid the question in a charitable sort of way.

"Bill Richards," he said. "One of my friends in Korea." He took off his glasses and rubbed at his tired eyes. "Not my best friend. But a good friend. A sweet guy. Not a mean bone in his body. Nineteen when he got killed. I woke up thinking about him. I've been alive all this time and he never had a chance. He was just getting started." He made a kind of waving gesture out at the yard, as if to indicate all the things in life that Bill Richards never got to experience.

He put his glasses back on. "When did that get so dirty?" he asked. His eyes had focused on the birdbath near the patio. "When did the birds decide to poop all over that?"

My father's become more philosophical and introspective since my mother died. He goes to daily Mass, and I go with him sometimes. He likes the 6:30 dawn special. The priest doesn't fart around at that hour; he gets the crew in and out in thirty minutes. Everybody there beside me is old, and they look beat up. With stiff hips they hobble up for communion. But I admire them. They endure. They go on.

My father sits down with us at the kitchen table, pulling up a chair between Len and me. "What were you talking about?"

6

Len pinches his lips shut. He clams up around my father. Afraid he'll give away his secret. That he's losing it again. My father's always the one who ends up signing the hospital papers.

"We were talking about the frontier days," I tell my father. "The Comanches."

"Oh," my father says, with the polite look of one not much interested in the subject. "That sure was a long time ago. Do you boys remember when this house was first built, all the mud instead of grass?"

"It wasn't so long ago, Dad," Len says with a quaver in his voice. "It wasn't so long ago. Do we have to pretend it never happened? Do we have to ignore the dead Indian on the table?"

My father blinks and squints at the table as if looking for the dead Indian, and Len's hand reaches out to clutch my father's robe near his throat. My father's pale, skinny chest seems to pulse. Len stares in wonder at the robe, running the fabric between his fingers. "That's the most beautiful robe I've ever seen, Dad."

My father chuckles. "This old thing?" But he sounds faintly pleased by the compliment.

Len's eyes mist over. "You're a beautiful man, Dad. You break my heart. You're Saint Francis of Assissi. I just want to take you in my arms and hold you."

My father draws his robe tighter about him, easing away from Len. "Say, let's have some pie," he says. "As long as we're up."

"That's a great idea, Dad." I follow him to the refrigerator. "Dad," I whisper, "I told you so. Len's having an episode."

My father leans in and out of the fridge and hands me an aluminum dish with some congealed peach pie in it. "Should we have some ice cream, too? Do you want to get some bowls, Kenneth?"

As my father ladles ice cream over the wedges of pie, Len's poised at the table. Listening. Watching us. Prepared to bolt.

We bring the bowls back to the table and my father sits between Len and me. "Didn't your mother have something about the Comanches in her roots stuff?" my father asks. "She used to love that old stuff, but I could never get very worked up about it. I wish I'd paid more attention to it now, for her sake."

"You're damn right she had stuff about the Comanches," Len says, his voice cracking with righteous indignation. "You're damn right she did! They came howling out of the hills, dragged Uncle Ira into the night, cut off his balls and staked him out on the plains."

My father swallows a big lump of pie. "My God," he says, "I never knew that."

"You had to read between the lines. They killed his wife and made off with his son. Uncle Ira survived. But he went crazy. He rode after them, became a vigilante. He did terrible things. Burned their villages. Killed women and children. He became a horror even to himself."

My father stares into space, holding his spoon in mid-air. Then he says, a little sadly, "Well, it was all a long time ago, Len."

"By the time they found the boy, nobody recognized him anymore. Even his own father. Even Uncle Ira. The boy didn't know where he belonged anymore. He had a raccoon for a pet, but it got rabies and died. Uncle Ira disappeared in the Gold Rush. The boy became an outlaw, then a sheriff, or he was a sheriff and then an outlaw. Mother wasn't clear about that. She always wanted a happy ending. Finally he just disappeared, too. You could read between the lines."

We look at Len and we realize there are tears splashed on his cheeks. My father touches Len's hand. "You miss your mother. I've been missing her too. All that roots stuff. It makes you think of her."

Len springs back from his touch, then smashes his fist down on the table. "Are you both out of your minds?" he screams at us. "Don't you understand anything I've been trying to tell you? Stop pretending you don't know what happened here!"

"My God, Len, easy, son," my father says. He reaches out to embrace Len, but Len shouts, "I will not abide it! This is an outrage! An outrage!"

He pushes my father away and runs out the sliding glass door into the backyard. We follow him into the thick heat of a full moon's summer night in Texas. My father raises his hand to his mouth and bites at the flesh between his thumb and index finger. "Oh God, not again," he mutters. "Not again." He puts out his hand, tries to catch up with Len, who has retreated towards the flowerbed at the far side of the lawn.

"Watch it, Dad, Len's got a knife."

"He wouldn't hurt us. He doesn't have a mean bone in his body."

"We've got to get him to the hospital, Dad, before something happens."

"Len?" my father shouts across the lawn. *"Len?"* His voice sounds like something cracking in two.

Len strides back and forth on the far side of the lawn, near the flowerbed. We cross the yard, huge shadows floating before us.

"Wow!" he says happily. "Fireflies!" He grabs our shoulders like a school kid with his buddies. "Look at all the fireflies, you guys! Don't you love fireflies? God, I love fireflies!"

My father and I look around as Len points. "There! Over there! Do you remember putting them in

9

jars, Kenneth? Putting them in jars in a dark room and they glowed?" He lightly punches my arm. "But you always made me let them go. You were so smart. You were so sensitive. God, I adore you. You're the best person I know. You are too, Dad. You're the best person I know. There's something sexy about you. I don't mean that in any weird sort of way."

My father rubs the side of his face, as if wondering if he's missed a shave. "I don't know why we don't have fireflies like we used to," he says. "We used to have fireflies all over the place, and we'd come out here, all of us, and your mother..."

Len chuckles as if listening to a child. "Don't be silly, Dad. We *still* have fireflies. Look at them! They're everywhere!"

My father and I stand in the warm, humid air. The yard looks much the same as always, the expanse of neat lawn, the flowerbed, the oak trees with their huge branches, the shrubs back by the alley, and the only thing amiss with the picture is that there aren't any fireflies. Not a one. If I were to paint the scene, I would have to imagine the fireflies.

"Don't you see them? Don't you *see* them?" He steps between us and looks desperately at us, as if we're playing a trick on him. "Are you guys blind?"

"Len," my father says heavily. He frowns down at his feet, his next words seeming to leak out of his mouth one by one. "We've got to do something about this, son."

Len recoils from us, making a cross with his fingers as if warding off a vampire. His shadow lengthens. As he whirls around to run, he stumbles and it gives me time to catch him. I try to tackle him, but he's twice as strong. He sends me flying. My father takes hold of his arm, but Len throws him to the ground. He pins my father's chest with his tennis-shoed foot. The knife comes out from underneath his shirt and he bends and holds it to my father's throat. "Don't make me kill you," he says. "Just ride off."

I ease myself towards them, afraid to come too fast. Afraid to startle him. I find my voice cracking. "Please, Len, it's Dad. It's Dad, Len."

He looks up at me, as if through a mesh screen, in the full moonlight blinking to get me in focus. His eyes fill with tears and he shudders and drops the knife, and I move in quickly to take it away and throw it up on the patio. He embraces my father, wedging his hands under my father's armpits and pulling him into a sitting position. "I'm sorry, Daddy. I'm sorry. Help me, Daddy. God help me."

"I will, son. I will." He cradles Len's head. "My sweet boy..."

"I can work through this, Daddy. Everything will be fine. You'll see. I'm playing golf in the morning. Just like old times. Like normal."

My father shakes his head, his voice coming out in a moan. "It's not normal, Len. Nothing's normal right now."

Len grips my father's arms, his blunt fingers digging into the flesh, his eyes wide and frightened. "I won't make it home this time, Daddy. Don't leave me there. Don't forget me."

My father's voice grows stronger. "We'll never forget you, Len. We'll make it home. I promise."

"I won't go back." He shoves my father away, and my father rocks back in the blue shadowed grass, thin pale legs beneath his bathrobe swinging up in the air like a rising see-saw.

I dive at Len, but he breaks for it. At the far side of the lawn, he springs nimbly over the chain-link fence into Mr. Robinson's back yard. My father sits up with a start, as if an alarm clock has blared in his ear. "The Doberman!" he cries.

Mr. Robinson's automatic floodlights click on and illuminate his yard. I help my father up and we hurry after Len to the fence, in time to see the Doberman, old Jeeter, seventeen now, go into his Hound of the Baskervilles' act. With the guttural snarl of an enraged drillmaster, he staggers stiff-legged across his turf. He's a horrid looking thing, with scabby patches of orange-tinted medicated fur. The old dinosaur moves on memory. One last glorious mission. One last neighborhood ass to chew.

As old Jeeter bares his teeth and hunches his shoulders to leap at Len, Len gives an ear splitting karate cry and launches a sidekick at Jeeter's head. He misses, but Jeeter yelps in fear. Tangling his legs in the retreat, Jeeter rolls like a flipped wrestler, but rage gives him youth and he springs back at Len, who yells, "Yow!" and breaks for the trampoline. He jumps up on it, and Jeeter yaps proudly as Mr. Robinson, in his bathrobe, perennial drink in hand, comes out on the flagstone patio. He observes Len bounce up and down on the trampoline, and he gives my father and me a friendly wave.

"Hoo boy," Mr. Robinson says with a chuckle. "Calm down, Jeeter, you old asshole. Don't give yourself a stroke."

Jeeter stops yapping, but he patrols the perimeter of the trampoline while Len bounds up and down, going higher and higher. "Hi there, Mr. Robinson," Len calls from mid-air.

"Howdy, Len. You know, I don't know if that old tramp will hold you any more. Mostly just the grandkids use it now." He pauses, cracks ice between his teeth. "Little guys."

Len tucks, lands on his butt, bounces back to his feet. "Feels okay."

Mr. Robinson chuckles. He's got a way of cracking ice in his teeth and talking at the same time.

"Glad to know it's held up. It just sits out in the rain. I think the kids oil the springs sometimes when they're in town."

"Hey there, John," my father calls. We lean over the chain-link fence and wave at Mr. Robinson.

"Hey there, Tom, Kenneth." While Jeeter stands guard over Len, Mr. Robinson joins us at the fence. His bathrobe, a thick, creamy beige, is in much better shape than my father's. He's a bullish looking man of seventy-two, with thick white calves beneath the robe.

My father clears his throat. "I'm mighty sorry to disturb you, John. We've got a kind of situation going on with Len again."

Mr. Robinson swings his head around to study Len bouncing high on the tramp, legs spread-eagled at the top of his flight. "I suspected that, Tom. Well, Len's welcome to bounce all night if it helps. Anything I can do?"

My father sighs. "Thank you, John. We're mighty obliged. He'll calm down and then we'll drive him to the hospital. He'll be ready to go."

"Come on over. Old Jeeter won't bite you. This has really sparked him up. He hasn't chased one of your boys in years."

I start to climb the fence and Mr. Robinson chuckles and cracks ice. "You can use the gate now, Ken."

We go out our side gate and through Mr. Robinson's gate into his yard and we shake hands. His big hand engulfs mine and my knuckles pop a little when he squeezes.

"How's Annie, John?" my father asks.

Mr. Robinson gets a tight sound in his throat. "Not so good, Tom. Not so good."

"I'm sorry to hear that."

He shrugs, the collar of his bathrobe shifting a little around his broad neck. "You know the score, Tom. You fellas want a drink?"

"No thanks, John. We'll just wait here."

"I'm going to check on Annie. She's restless tonight."

Mr. Robinson goes inside to check on his wife. I eye old Jeeter, but he looks nervous to be left alone with us. He retreats to the patio and hides under the swinging bench.

"Look at this!" Len calls. He bounces high and turns a flip, landing neatly on his feet.

"My God, Len, don't do that," my father says. "Do you want to hurt yourself?"

"I'm good," Len says. "Aren't I good?"

"Sure. But you don't need to prove anything."

"Drumroll please." He launches another flip. He stumbles as he lands, running forward a couple of steps, but stopping before he falls. "Tuh dah!" He holds his arms aloft, the Olympic winner on display.

Mr. Robinson appears with a fresh drink. "Len, you're going to give my insurance agent a fit."

Len talks to my father as he bounces. "How come you didn't give me gymnastics lessons when I was a kid? I could have amounted to something."

"I didn't know you wanted gymnastics lessons."

"I did, but I just didn't know it back then."

"Would you like to come down and have a scotch, Len?" Mr. Robinson asks. He cracks ice. "Or maybe some milk? Buttermilk? Maybe we got some old buttermilk around here, in a jar someplace. I fancy a nice cold drink of buttermilk now and then myself..." He frowns at his glass, jostles the liquid around a little and murmurs, "Though this works in a pinch."

"I could have been a flying Wallenda!" The springs creak in the old trampoline as Len flies higher

14

and higher. He pulls his knees up, tucks his head to flip.

"No, Len!" my father cries.

He doesn't get all the way around, but crashes on his neck and shoulder. He lets out a moan and curls into a ball.

"Len!" Dad shouts. "Are you hurt, son?"

"Aw hell, Tom, you're going to clean me out," Mr. Robinson says with profound resignation. "I'll call my insurance agent. There goes the boat." He sighs, shakes the ice in his glass around. "Shit. I wanted to leave something to the kids."

I jump on the trampoline to help Len, but he rolls over the springs to the ground. Clutching his neck like a man waking up with a terrific charley horse, he lurches over the lawn, falls into the swimming pool, and sinks straight to the bottom.

I do a moonwalk to the other side of the tramp and jump hard to the ground, falling and skinning my knees. As I pull my T-shirt over my head, my father pinches my arms with skinny strong fingers. "Don't! He'll drag you down!" He kneels on the edge of the pool and puts his face near the water and shouts, "Get up here right now, Len! I mean it!"

"I've got a long pole here someplace," Mr. Robinson says. "A cleaning net. I think I can hook him."

I jump in, feet first. When I sink down to the bottom, I see Len doing a kind of underwater ballet act. In a bluish light, he pirouettes, spreads his arms, operatic, Romeo beckoning to Juliet. His hair's blown back in the water. When he sees me, his eyes widen as if a fearsome creature has swum into God's glorious lagoon. He slugs me in the jaw and leaps on me. A long pole pokes into the back of my neck and a net wraps around my face. Len gets me in a headlock and kicks us toward the surface. He's seventeen again. A

15

lifeguard once more. The best in the neighborhood.
The best everything.

He drags me out and throws me on the tiles
bordering the pool. He frees my face from the cleaning
net, begins to administer CPR, but then jumps back in
horror. His finger traces the long scar on my chest from
my heart surgery when I was a child.

"They cut his heart out!" he shrieks.

As Len runs for the street side of the corner lot,
Jeeter streaks out from under the swinging bench like a
torpedo released from its chute. Len's a step ahead as
he hits the fence. He leaps to hurdle it and howls as he
lands. He's caught on the fence, straddling it, while
Jeeter gnaws at his jeans. Len topples free and limps
into the night, running beneath the full moon, a crazed
scout turned loose on the neighborhood.

Mr. Robinson holds his cleaning net like a
lance. "Well, this has been a hell of a night," he says.

He leads us to the gate. Old Jeeter struts behind.
He growls low in his throat, gives me a last malevolent
glare. Next time, punk, he warns. Next time.

Mr. Robinson shakes my father's hand. "Good
luck, Tom. Come back for a drink sometime. Don't be
a stranger, Ken."

An apparition appears on the lawn. A woman
all in white, aglow in the moonlight.

"Are the boys home?" a trembling voice calls.
"Is it the boys?" She opens her arms to us, her white
nightgown full of billowy loose folds.

"Oh hell," Mr. Robinson mutters. "Go inside,
Annie," he calls. "Go inside." He gives me a sudden,
forceful hug, drawing me into a thick neck scented with
aftershave. "Go find him, Kenneth. *Find him!*"

He ushers us out the gate and turns to comfort
his wife. She's on her knees, sobbing near the
trampoline, and he lifts her gently under the arms and
leads her inside.

We back my father's sedan out of the garage. I drive in my wet clothes, and my father pulls his bathrobe tighter about his throat.

We prowl the neighborhood. It's a nicely established neighborhood now, new when I was growing up, a mix of ranch and two-story brick houses. One house up the block has white columns in front, but it has always stood out as pretentious.

We catch glimpses of Len hiding behind trees, darting down alleyways. Our headlights zoom in on him as he crouches behind some trash cans. He shields his eyes with his arm, then runs.

He crosses Bandera Road into a rough part of town. Shotgun homes. Peeling paint. Broken machinery in the yards. The oaks and willows press hard to the road, branches untrimmed, and our lights sweep into the shrubbery alongside the houses, probe into the secret places.

A new brick apartment building has gone up. It has a gentrified look, an attempt to reclaim this part of town. But a keg party's underway on the balustrade and revelers spill in and out of open doorways.

My father adjusts the flaps of his robe over his thighs. "When did this all happen?" he asks. "When did it all happen?"

Our headlights catch up with Len as he races across a weedy, vacant lot. Deer-like, he freezes a moment before sprinting off again, and for a moment I feel like I enter his world. One oak ahead in the distance. A lone runner on the prairie, arms raised to take an arrow in the back, the hooves of the horses pounding after him.

The Real World

One early afternoon in May, my friend Tom Donahue, owner of *Flushright,* a one man sewer and drain cleaning company, called to ask me if I would help him on a job. When I asked him what I would be doing, he was vague. "Trust me, Jim. You'll enjoy it. This line of work is fascinating, and you'll have the opportunity to watch a real pro in action."

He named a modest hourly wage and I accepted. I couldn't afford to be too choosy. I'd gotten out of college a couple of years before, during the recession of the early 1980's, and I worked at a restaurant and at various odd jobs, but it was difficult to make ends meet. Currently, I was living in the garage of some friends of mine. The rent was low and they'd said I could stay as long as I wanted, but they'd need to park their car in the garage when winter came. It was a small car, though, and I was hoping I could adjust.

When Tom honked, I ran out of the garage to meet him, and when I got in the blue van and slammed the door, Tom flinched and put a hand to his ear. "Easy on the door of the Blue Bullet, Jim. People all over Santa Fe are counting on us. We're the last line of defense between them and disaster."

"How can you bear the burden?"

"Nerves of steel. Provided I eat. At the moment I'm having a low blood sugar attack, but we don't have time for lunch."

A man on a mission, he drove fast but not recklessly, his eyes staring beyond the traffic on Guadalupe Street, to the piney foothills of the Sangre de Cristo mountains. The traffic was an encumbrance, but he had learned to be tolerant. "Aye, laddie," he said, feigning an Irish brogue. "This be a hot fair day, 'tis,

18

perfect for sewering." He drank coffee from a huge styrofoam cup, lit a cigarette, and began to speak glowingly of the joys of sewer and drain cleaning, of the limitless opportunities for rugged, resourceful individuals. He glanced sidelong at me. "But it takes soul," he said.

Tom was a husky fellow, thirty-two, with curly dark hair that stuck out farther on one side than the other. He had blue eyes, a sunburned nose, and black fingernails. Like your stereotypical plumber, he always seemed to be wearing a dirty T-shirt and soiled jeans that hung low and exposed the crack of his ass. But he wasn't stereotypical. Tom's dream was to be a playwright, though he was supporting his family as a sewer and drain cleaner. He'd gone into the field reluctantly, but in recent months he'd been speaking fondly of the small businessman's contributions to society.

We traveled into a neighborhood of large old adobe houses, drove down a long dirt driveway, and parked in front of a sprawling house with a stucco wall surrounding it, creating a fortress-like atmosphere. Tom puffed thoughtfully on his cigarette. "Yes, lad, today you'll learn a little of the philosophy behind sewer and drain cleaning. You won't understand half of what we're doing, but one day when you most need it, the knowledge will come back to you."

"Why would I need it?"

He beamed at me like a father surprising his son with a new bicycle. "Jim, I brought you along for a reason today." He reached a strong hand out and settled it on my shoulder. "I want you to go into business with me. At first you'll serve an apprenticeship. I can't afford to pay you a lot during training, but I'll be there every step of the way. I won't send you into anything you can't handle. When you're ready to fly on your own, I'll turn the Blue Bullet over

19

to you and you'll do the fieldwork while I handle customer relations. You'll make forty percent of everything you make on your calls." He studied my wide-eyed expression and his own eyes narrowed. "Eventually it will be forty-five percent. Maybe fifty, we can talk."

"It's not the percentage, Tom. I'm sure that's very generous."

He squeezed my shoulder. "You're a little frightened. That's natural. I'd be worried if you weren't."

"I don't know anything about plumbing."

He sat back and chuckled, as if he had heard this faulty line of reasoning a thousand times before. "This isn't *plumbing.* It's sewer and drain cleaning. It's less of a science than an art. It's an instinctive thing."

"Tom, I appreciate the offer, I really do. But I wouldn't be any good at it. I don't have any mechanical aptitude."

"You don't *need* any mechanical aptitude." He tapped his chest in the vicinity of his heart. "It's here. This is where it all starts. You're a natural."

"Well, I don't know," I said.

"That's the right attitude. Always start with doubt. Don't even believe your customer right off. There may be nothing wrong with his drain at all. Maybe he's imagining things. Sometimes you've got to come down hard, tell him to plunge it himself." Tom sighed expansively. "I was exactly like you once. I hid out in my room, putting my pathetic little thoughts down on paper. Then I became a man of action. Once you get over your fear of the real world, you'll love this work. You'll never want to go back."

From the consul, he picked up a baseball cap and sunglasses. With the dark shades and the brim of the hat tucked low, he resembled a jaded undercover cop. "Let's go for it. No guts, no glory."

Following orders, I got a pick and shovel out of the rear of the van and the man of action hitched up his baggy jeans and led us around the side of the house and into the backyard. A tall, thin, balding man came out of the house to meet us. He was wearing Bermuda shorts and drinking sun tea out of an impressively large glass. Tom gripped the tall man's arms as if they were old friends. "I set everything aside to come back, Mr. Gorman. This time, I've brought along my apprentice, Jim." Mr. Gorman and I shook hands. It was a hot, blue, dry afternoon, and for a moment we all stood quietly in the yard.

"Do you fellows think you can fix it today?" Mr. Gorman asked. "I thought you had it yesterday, and then the toilet overflowed again this morning. Everything was fine last night."

Tom nodded. "That was last night. Today's a new ballgame. We're dealing with a labyrinth here. It's the most complex piping I've ever seen. If this doesn't work, we'll probably have to get in a backhoe, knock out the walls and take down some trees. Every toilet in there is a ticking time bomb. The offset lines could erupt and bring the whole place down."

Mr. Gorman stared at the house. A shiver seemed to pass through his shoulders.

"We're not going to let that happen, Mr. Gorman. Not on my watch." Tom described a course of action, something about a tank that we were going to unearth. Steering Mr. Gorman by the elbow, he led us both deeper into the backyard. He tapped the ground with his boot. "Dig here, Jim. Your apprenticeship begins." He gave me the thumbs up to show me I was his man.

"Life will soon look a lot rosier around here," Tom said.

"I sure hope so. My wife is taking it hard."

Tom took the shovel from me and nodded at the pick. "Start with that." From the rear pocket of his jeans, he pulled out a pair of grimy work gloves. "Here, put these on. You haven't toughened your hands yet."

I put the gloves on, took a good hold of the pick, said, "Look out, gentlemen." I expanded my chest with a deep breath, raised the pick over my head and gave a mighty downward stroke. Painful vibrations ran through my hands and up my arms, and I saw that I had dislodged a tiny piece of soil from the planet. Tom frowned. Mr. Gorman stared at the barely dented earth. "The ground's always hard at first," I said. "From the winter snows."

I carried on for a few more minutes, but the soil was rocky and soon I was sweaty and exhausted and I only seemed to have created a semi-circle of shallow craters in the ground. I stepped back, panting. Tom and Mr. Gorman looked disappointed. "I think I've accomplished some things here," I said, "but at this point we may need some sort of trenching machine."

"Let me see that pick," Tom said.

He picked with rapid, vigorous strokes, heaving his considerable weight into it. The soil fell away in large clumps, but then he bent over, red-faced, gasping for breath. He pushed the pick back at me. "I think you were too tentative," he wheezed. "Use a little more body English."

I picked and shoveled the loose dirt out, picked and shoveled. Sweat rolled down my face, but my breathing evened out as I hit my rhythm. A woman and two nice-looking small children, a boy and a girl, came out of the house and stood beside Tom and Mr. Gorman. The children held onto Mrs. Gorman's legs. She held two large glasses of iced tea. She handed Tom a glass and glanced at me. "For you and your friend," she said in a kind voice.

Tom took the second glass from her hands. "He'll have his break later. He doesn't like to drink when he works."

As he quaffed both glasses of tea, Tom explained to the Gorman family that the pipes were of a low-grade material that was used during the forties because all the iron was going to the war effort.

"Fascinating," Mr. Gorman said. "You really know your stuff."

Tom referred again to the labyrinth of piping and led the Gormans off on an inspection. They disappeared around the side of the house.

I kept digging and the hole grew deeper, until I saw a glint of metal in the ground. I set my shovel down and toured the perimeter of the house, looking for Tom. I heard voices and I peered through a window and saw Tom and the Gormans sitting at a sunny table in the kitchen. They had switched to milk and apple pie. I tapped on the window and they all turned their heads and waved like a cheerful scout troop. I went back to the hole and picked some more and after a while Tom and the Gormans came out of the house and stood near me. "How's it going?" Tom asked. "Why'd you stop?"

"I saw some metal down there."

Tom and the Gormans stared down at the widened hole. "You did good," Tom said. "That's the top of the tank right there."

"What's next?" I asked.

"We're almost there, where the pipe feeds into the tank. Go carefully."

I picked and shoveled some more.

"Easy now." Tom squatted on his haunches to observe.

I stroked downward with the pick once more and heard the sound of metal striking metal. "I think we're home," I said.

Tom sighed wearily. "No. I think you just broke the pipe."

Mr. Gorman's voice quavered. "The pipe's broken?"

Peering from behind his mother's leg, the little boy said sadly, "Where will we pee now?"

His mother pressed a comforting hand to the top of his head, though in her slumped shoulders, I saw the beginnings of despair as if she, too, wondered where they would pee from now on.

"In a way, this is just as good," Tom said. "We can feed the snake in here and then patch the pipe."

Tom rolled a machine from the van, a coiled metal snake with blades at the end. He fed the snake into the pipe and the blades bit at the thick roots. I lay down in the hole and pulled out the tangled gunk the blades kicked up. The hole filled with backwash and muck, and I was covered from head to foot in a foul-smelling slime. I breathed through my mouth, gagging. I rolled on my side and glanced up at the Gorman family, who were like apparitions, impossibly clean, ready for a day at the tennis club.

Above me, Tom knelt on the edge of the hole, and he ordered me to roll out of the way so he could feed the snake in a few more inches. "Now this doesn't happen often," he warned, "but if the snake jumps, lie completely still and cover your head."

Mr. Gorman seemed calmer now, anticipating a return to normalcy. Ooze from the pipe squirted me in the face, and as I wiped the gunk away, he said, "So you're the apprentice."

"He's a natural," Tom said. "It just takes a little getting used to the real world."

"It doesn't get any realer than this," Mr. Gorman said.

"The snake's starting to really chew," Tom said. "You can get out now."

24

I crawled from my slimy coffin as the Gormans crinkled their noses and moved upwind. "Yuck," the little girl said. Mrs. Gorman put her arms over her children's shoulders and ushered them toward the house. Mr. Gorman remained, looking on, a tall solitary man biting his lip.

"You did good," Tom said, as he finished running the snake through the line. "A lot of guys won't go down in the hole like that."

Tom recoiled the snake and wiped sweat from his forehead. He patched the pipe and nodded at the shovel. "Throw a little dirt back in the hole."

Tom turned and grinned at Mr. Gorman. "I think your troubles are over. But we'd better check it out inside."

"So you've got it beat?"

"You don't beat this sewer system, Mr. Gorman. You only pacify it for a while."

Mr. Gorman laughed. They walked shoulder to shoulder to the house, and the children came out and jumped up and down and cheered. Mrs. Gorman handed Tom another glass of tea and kissed him on the cheek.

I finished covering up the hole, and when Tom came out we loaded up the van and he handed me a soiled towel. "Here, wipe yourself off a little before you get in."

We shot the Blue Bullet back into traffic. "Thank God, now we can eat," Tom said. "The last time I skipped lunch, I backed my van into an arroyo."

As we drove, he rhapsodized about our future together, the solid income, the hard physical work, the satisfaction of helping people.

"I don't think it's for me," I said.

His head angled toward me, and there was a dangerous glitter in his eyes. "You think this kind of work is beneath you. You think it's dirty."

"Not at all, Tom. It has its charms."

"I think it's terrible that you live in a garage. What about a family? What about a useful role in society? I used to be just like you. Lost in my head. I sat in my room writing plays that nobody cared about. People care if I make the water go down. If you make the water go down, they think you're a saint. Don't waste your life, Jim. Join the real world."

"What is the real world?" I asked.

The beeper on his belt went off, emitting high-pitched bleeps. "That is," he said. "That's the real world calling." He swerved into the parking lot of a convenience store, hopped out of the van and talked urgently into the pay phone as I got out to buy a Coke.

"Stop!" he shouted, hanging up the phone. "We don't have time. Get back in."

"I want a Coke."

"We've got to go back to the Gorman's. Coke will bloat you."

"I'm thirsty."

"All right," he snapped. "But hurry, and buy me one while you're at it. I've got to raise my blood sugar."

We chugged our sodas and sped back to the Gorman's. Mrs. Gorman opened the front door and said quietly, "He's taking it hard." She led us upstairs to the elegant bathroom in the master bedroom where Mr. Gorman waited, staring at the toilet and the soggy towels on the while tile floor. "It happened again," he said dully.

"Easy, Mr. Gorman," Tom said. "Tell me exactly what happened. Start from the beginning."

"Well," Mr. Gorman said. "About two weeks ago, we were just back from a trip to Taos when I came upstairs and the first thing I-"

"I mean what happened just now," Tom said. "Did the water swirl first, or did it just rise and gush over the top?"

Mr. Gorman closed his eyes in thought. "I think it swirled."

"You're sure? It swirled?"

"Well, I'm pretty sure it swirled, but it wouldn't swoosh down."

Tom nodded. "This is good," he said.

"It is?"

"I don't think we're talking about a line problem any more. This is more on the surface. Jim, get me the tool box and the auger out of the van, and there's a box with a valve in it. I'm going to replace the valve and raise the water pressure. I think that will give us the swoosh we're looking for."

When I brought the equipment back, Tom told me to pay attention. He twisted the auger into the toilet bowl. "This is the way you check for calcium deposits."

"So how does it feel to be the apprentice?" Mr. Gorman asked. "At least you'll never be replaced by a computer."

Tom installed the new valve and raised the water pressure. He unraveled toilet paper, dropped it into the bowl and flushed. We all held our breaths as the water swirled, rose a few inches, and then swooshed down.

Mr. Gorman let out a breath. "I guess that's it then." He laughed. "This calls for champagne," he said. "Seriously, you fellows must be ready for a beer." He giggled, a little giddily. "Really, you know, I've been feeling a little like shooting you. No offense."

"Well, that won't be necessary now," Tom said, chuckling a little himself, but catching my eye warily. I sensed that others had snapped on him in the past.

My shoulder touched Mr. Gorman's. There was a nice feeling of comraderie in the bathroom, a sense of shared victory. To make sure, Tom dropped another handful of paper into the toilet and flushed again. We watched the water swirl up, rise inch by inch until it lapped over the edge of the toilet and streamed over the towels as we retreated to the door of the bathroom.

"My God," Mr. Gorman whispered hoarsely.

"I'm not going to charge you anything for this return visit, Mr. Gorman," Tom said. "I think I understand the problem now."

Tom led us down the stairs and into the yard once again, toward the spot where we'd dug the hole earlier in the afternoon. "I didn't run enough line in earlier," he said to me. "I saw that you were getting antsy. I shouldn't have let your mood affect my judgment."

I picked and he shoveled as we dug the hole again. In grim silence, Mr. Gorman looked on. Tom's beeper went off, and he removed it from his belt and stared at it. For a moment I thought he might throw the beeper, but he only turned it off and set it on the ground. His face was red and his breath was ragged as he glanced at the sun, which was getting low on the horizon. We broke into the pipe and ran the snake through until it was almost completely uncoiled. Then Tom recoiled the snake and he went down into the hole to patch the pipe. When he came out, he brushed mud from the knees of his jeans and looked at Mr. Gorman with bloodshot eyes. "That's it," he said. "That's all I can do."

Mr. Gorman shook his head. "I've been living in a fool's paradise."

"We all are, Mr. Gorman. We all are." They left me to fill in the hole and as they walked inside to check the toilet, their shoulders bumped together like old soldiers.

I was almost finished filling in the hole when I noticed Tom's beeper on the ground. I stood over it with a shovel of dirt. It was tempting to bury that beeper, to save Tom from its clarion call to duty. Tom was right about one thing. Sewer and drain cleaners really were lonely saints of the underworld, engaged in a noble battle.

But something had gone seriously wrong with this mission, and saints are reviled when they don't come through. I saw Tom slinking out of the house, uncharacteristically sheepish, back canted forward, head ducked, hands raised to his ears as if to ward off bitter words. The Gorman clan spilled out of the house, fast behind him, and Mr. Gorman, who had been the soul of gentility all day, whose voice had never risen, who had never questioned a major decision, now drew himself up to full height and cried in a high-pitched, enraged voice, "Bastards! What have you done? Bastards!" A moment later, Mrs. Gorman, who had been a veritable angel of sympathy, shouted, "Clean up this mess! We're *suing!*" The children showered Tom's fleeing back with marbles.

The man of action swept past me, muttering, "Let's go. Hurry. Hurry. *Run!*" Tom's retreat swept me up and we bolted for the van as if pursued by a wall of rushing water. In the twilight, jogging with pick in one hand, shovel in the other, I glanced back and saw the Gormans scattering across the lawn, as if panicked, as if driven from their home by something beastly that had occurred inside. We dove into the Blue Bullet, driving in stunned silence, the accusatory voices of the Gormans seeming to hover between us, until Tom left the dirt roads and merged back into the reassuring world of concrete streets, the thickening traffic seeming to calm him. He lit a cigarette and drank the remains of a leftover cup of cold coffee. "This may have been a little rough for your first day, but it doesn't usually end

29

like that. While we were working upstairs, their whole system failed. Everything shot back up the main drain and it spread down the hallway like lava. But at least a portion of the house is still livable. We're going to have to lay low for a while, work the east side of town, do a couple of easy clogged sinks." He lit another cigarette off the burning embers of the last one, and passed it to me, and even though I wasn't a smoker, I puffed on it, trying it on for feel.

All I could think of, though, was getting back to my humble garage, where I could shut myself in, turn on my lamp, open my notebook, and scribble myself into another world entirely, a world some thought not real at all. The voices of the Gormans lingered, though, and I could not block off the vision of a backhoe plowing through their trees, roaring angrily as it unearthed the labyrinth beneath.

Excellence

I'm not after excellence in the Tai Chi classes I teach. I'm happy if nobody falls. I teach the geriatrics classes down at the community hospital, and my students are a fragile crew, with replacement hips, osteoporosis, shot knees, and swollen gall bladders.

It's okay by me. I'm no great shakes myself. I've gotten a little heavy, a little gray in the beard. My digestion's off and my flatulence wafts through our therapy gym like a reminder of death. All through our classes I rhapsodize about balance and harmony, yin and yang, the glories of chi energy, but I swig coffee all the way to my morning classes and tonight after my evening classes, I'll get drunk.

You've heard the story before. Man goes to seed. Loses his wife and kids. Man goes more to seed.

I knew excellence once. Maybe I didn't have it myself, but I came close to it, close enough to touch.

Master Wu—he didn't want to be called that, but it was hard not to think of him that way—sometimes pulled me aside while one of his more advanced students led the class.

"Stand there," he said once, in my first year at the school. "Don't move."

"Okay." I was already beat from the earlier workout, but I got into my front stance, assumed the Single Whip posture with my right arm out to the side, my hand bent at the wrist, forming a hook. I bent my knees. Sank my weight. Settled into the hardwood floor of the studio. Master Wu walked slowly around me, frowning, observing me from different angles as if examining a recalcitrant show horse. I half expected him to check my teeth. Master Wu was seventy, but he could pass for fifty. His skin was nearly free of

31

wrinkles and his eyes gleamed. His hair was a glossy black. I was twenty-seven, but I had dark circles under my eyes. I already had a drinking problem. As I held the posture sweat ran down my cheeks and my quads burned. A cool summer evening breeze floated off the Alameda lagoon and drifted through the open side door. I glanced with sadness at the fading light. If Master Wu turned, I'd bolt and make for a bar. If I could still move.

With a sharp finger, he poked me in the chest, near my heart. "Relax here. Too stiff." He sighed. "Sink lower."

"Really?" My legs screamed in pain. "I'm pretty low already."

"Be like a tree."

"What kind?"

"Rooted."

"Okay."

"Grounded."

"Right."

"What happens when a wind blows the tree?"

I furrowed my brow. It was hard to concentrate. My legs were doing a skittery little St. Vitus's dance on the floor, which was slick from my sweat.

"You don't know?"

"Not at the moment."

"Hm," he said. He often said "hm" when he wasn't pleased. I wasn't one of his favorites. He thought me arrogant among other things. I'd studied karate for a few years and I imagined myself a bit of a tough guy. Also, I had a habit of popping up from the painful crouched positions for a quick breather whenever I thought he wasn't looking. He'd caught me a couple of times and had given me sinister looks.

"The wind blows the branches," he said. "What then?"

"They rustle?"

He stared at me. "They do what?"

"Rustle? Kind of shake?"

"Ah." He smiled. "Like your legs."

"I suppose so."

His eyes bore in on me, two glittery daggers. "When the wind blows the trees, the branches move. Left, right, up, down, front, back. They move."

He took a short, bitter breath. He was not the sort to say "asshole", but his exhalation seemed to take the place of the word. They *move,* asshole.

"If they don't move, the branches break. Too stiff. Too much resistance."

Perhaps Master Wu was not fond of me because he had read my mind. I towered over him, held a sixty pound advantage. With my legs screaming, I thought of smacking him.

"Okay, they move," I gritted through my teeth. "They move, gotcha."

"Hm." He licked his finger, lifted it as if to test the wind. "Which way does the wind blow?"

"I have no fuc-...I have no idea. But I hope we can figure it out soon."

"Which way?"

"South?"

"South?" His eyes widened in amazement. "You say south?"

"North?"

Something criminal flashed in his eyes. "North? South? What are you talking about?"

"I don't know. What are *you* talking about?"

"Which way does the wind blow?" He made a motion with his eyes toward his wind-testing finger.

"Wherever it wants," I said. I was a thread away from falling over now.

"Ah. And the trunk?"

I took a stab at it. "The trunk doesn't move? It's rooted?"

His eyes lit up. He patted me on the back. "Yes. Good. Yes. The branches move, they follow the wind, but the trunk doesn't move. Rooted. Grounded. Nothing fake."

"Okay," I said. "I got it."

"You got it?"

'Yeah. I got it."

He gave me a gentle push on the chest then; his hands seemed light as feathers, yet I found myself sailing back into the mattress which hung on the wall for such purposes. I slid to the floor. He helped me up, kind of dusted me off, gave me a friendlier, kinder smile. "Of course sometimes a wind can knock down even a big, strong tree."

I stuck around the studio though. I stayed for several years, attended classes three nights per week. My legs got strong, my form wasn't bad. I learned to sink my chi to the tan tien, a point just below the navel. Yet, something was missing. I wasn't getting it. I elicited many "hms" from Master Wu.

He did not want us to bow to him, and he preferred we call him by his first name, Andrew, the name given to him in a missionary school in China when he was a boy. I felt false, though, when I called him by his first name, so after a while I avoided using his name entirely.

I wanted to please him. Perversely, I also wanted to *not* please him. He laughed and joked naturally with many of the students. With me, something always came up, something hard rose between us. I wanted more from him, I wanted less. Resentments crept in. I resisted him one day, became slavish the next, forgot myself, made grand bows of devotion one day, said something smart-ass the next.

One day I was Pushing Hands with a fellow student who'd been at the studio about as long as I had.

In Push Hands the idea is to keep your own balance while pushing your partner off balance, using as little force as possible. You have to be rooted, yet soft and yielding, too. You have to listen with your hands for the opening to your partner's center. You can't stiffen up or resist. At its finest, Push Hands feels more like a splendid dance than a competition. Nobody loses, everyone wins. But I was bigger and stronger than most of the people in class and if good principles wouldn't work for me, I'd often resort to brute strength.

This particular day, I felt Master Wu's eyes on my partner and me. I didn't want to be pushed out with him watching, so I started using my full force and weight against my smaller opponent. He put up a valiant defense, but pretty soon I was shoving him all over the place as he grew sweaty, tired, and humiliated. Yet I kept on, aware that I was hurting a friend. I hated myself for it, but I couldn't stop myself. It was all I could do to keep from picking up the poor fellow and tossing him through a window. Or perhaps I'd fling him up and catch his sweatshirt on the ceiling fan and do a victory dance as he spun helplessly round and round. The ceiling fan toss would become legendary. I was in a chi frenzy, my fire element overloaded. The hell with soft and yielding, I wanted to throw people. Come at me! I will throw, throw, *throw* you! Through windows, to the ceiling, out the door! You too Master Wu! Everyone out, out, out, until I stand alone, lasers of chi energy shooting out my fingertips, the new Master of the studio.

Master Wu looked on, appalled, waiting to see just how far I would go. Finally he stepped in and touched my friend's shoulder. "Very good," he said soothingly. "You followed the principles. Don't worry. One day it will be different."

Master Wu pulled me aside, walked me over a few feet so we could talk alone.

"What's wrong?" I asked. "I was winning, wasn't I?"

"Two things wrong," he said. "Need to relax. And bad attitude. Don't worry about winning. Invest in loss."

He looked at me in a new way. There was no challenge in his look, no anger, no put down. It was a sad and resigned look. Maybe it was the look of a doctor offering a cancer diagnosis to his patient. Relax, I knew meant something different to him. Relax in the most profound way, letting go of fear, worry, anger, pretension, a bloated self-image.

"Fix those things," he said sadly, as if I never would. "And you can be great."

He walked away. I have many images of his trim back receding. He never appeared to be hurrying, but in a few blinks of the eye he glided across the hardwood floor, arriving in time to correct yet another Tai Chi aberration.

When I told Master Wu—Andrew—I was leaving California, I think he was relieved. Then I told him my girlfriend Annie was coming with me. We'd met in class. Her energy flowed right, she was loose, happy, balanced. She was one of Andrew's favorites, one of the students he joked and laughed with naturally.

"Hm," he said. He paused. "Well, good luck."

On my last night of class, though, he gave me a book wrapped in brown paper. I didn't look at it until later, riding home on the BART. I'd expected a Tai Chi book, but it was one of Thomas Merton's. I set it aside somewhere and didn't read it for a number of years.

A lot of life went by. Annie and I bounced around at first, then she went to medical school. We settled down, had kids. I taught Tai Chi classes and hung out with the kids while she built up her practice. The kids and I had a ball, but I let myself slide. I got lazy. I coasted. I couldn't compete with Annie's success, so I stopped trying.

The last couple of years I took to watching too much T.V. when I should have been training or spending time with the family. I watched baseball and basketball, and in football season, all the games I could find on Saturday, Sunday, Monday night. You see the players get knocked out of the game, you see the knees twist in gruesome ways where you know the player will never be the same. The camera zooms in on the guy writhing in pain and I think: that's me, that awaits.

I did a couple of stupid things this last year. First, I fell in love. Nothing came of it, it was all whimsical, but my would-be-lover lay in bed between Annie and me like a tangible presence. She seemed so real and close sometimes, I felt like feeding her grapes. The unrequited, unspoken of love dropped my spirits into the Great Abyss, an energetic point located, I believe, somewhere between the shoulder blades.

The worst thing was this. My mother died a few months before and shortly after, after ten years dry, I started drinking again. I won't say it was cause and effect, but perhaps my mother's death gave me the nudge I was looking for. Annie steered me toward counseling and A.A. I went through the motions, but dropped deeper.

I wasn't good to live with any more. Our house suffered from aggressive energy. I didn't want the kids to see me drinking. Annie and I agreed it would be best if I moved into a little apartment.

I know now I've missed some essential lesson. My chi seems to be flowing backwards. I've lost my root, my branches flail and break off in the wind. I need to go back, to regroup. Sometimes I dream myself back to the studio. I'm pushing hands with Master Wu. Our movements are light, graceful, smooth. We smile at one another. In his eyes, I see love. You, you are the one after all, the eyes say, you will be the embodiment of my teachings. *This is the secret, now I will reveal all,* and he begins to whisper as I cock my head to listen...But the dream is never fulfilled, always flitters into the absurd. Master Wu suspended from the ceiling fan, spinning above me, chortling, or the Alameda lagoon rising up in a tidal wave, sweeping through the studio while we scamper for the roof. Fires erupt, sword fights break out. Annie kneels over the wounded, taking blood pressures, the kids clutch at my trousers...I need to go back, but Andrew is dead now. An aneurism.

What I think about life now is not profound, but it is this: it breaks us. No matter how strong we think we are. All at once, suddenly, or bit by bit. It gets us. It's a sad enterprise, life. Lovely, too, don't get me wrong. But we falter. The steam comes off the fastball, the slider doesn't sink, the curve ball hangs too long over the plate.

"Sit down! When you're tired, sit down! Please sit down!" I exhort my seniors at the hospital. "Don't push it!"

They come at me with their steel knees, their plastic hips. Dottie's on oxygen, John has a metal plate in his head. "I hear things," he says. "Will this help?" It's an accomplishment if we all face the same wall.

"Don't push it! Sit if you're tired!"

Is this what the football coaches yell at their players? Don't push it, boys, let the other guys get all sweaty if they want, we're going to go at our own pace.

Still, there are breakthroughs. Marilyn's bone density increases. George's balance improves enough so that he can stand on one leg to slip on his trousers. John feels the chi in the top of his head.

And sometimes, as we shift our weight back and forth, back and forth, like the gentle back and forth of a rocking chair, as our joints creak along with the hardwood floor, sometimes, just sometimes, I feel like we're all getting there together, getting along, going to make it to the promised land of chi. And sometimes, maybe, in our own slow, plodding, faltering way, as the wall clock ticks over our heads, in the very thick of our mediocrity, we touch excellence.

A couple of weeks ago, I found a little chapel in the hospital where I teach. I like to sit in the back pew when the chapel is quiet and empty. I try to pray. Not too well maybe. I think what I need to do is to let go, to let God talk to me instead of trying to talk to God. I've got to stop trying to impress God. I've got to stop performing.

There was a fire in our house, in the kitchen. Annie and the kids are staying in a hotel while repairs are made.

I go over to visit them. I bring Chinese food for Annie, Happy Meals for the kids. I've been sober twelve days. Feeling good. That curious calm after the storm. But tentative too. Vulnerable. Shaky.

The kids hop all over me, we wrestle from bed to bed. After a while, they lose interest. They watch the cartoons.

Annie sits on the edge of one bed as we eat. I sit on the other bed so that our knees almost touch. We look at each other. I shrug. She shrugs. We sigh.

I stand up, set aside my carton of fried rice. "Push me," I say. I assume the Ward Off Left, offer my forearm.

She laughs. But she stands, pushes against my elbow and wrist. She's always had the edge, the natural softness and root. My back muscles stiffen, the old hard force rises up. But then I drop my tailbone, turn my waist. I yield. I follow her lead until it becomes a kind of dance, her leading, then me leading, rocking back and forth, turning our waists and hips, until you can't tell any more who's leading and who's following, until we don't know where we're going or where we've been.

All of a sudden she shoulder-strikes me in the stomach and knocks me down on the bed. She collapses beside me. We lie on our backs, staring up at the ceiling. "I'm sorry," she says.

I hold my belly. "Did that help?"

"Yes. Thanks. I feel better now."

Her hand strays over to mine. "Are you okay?"

"I don't know."

"What do you need?"

I settle into the mattress, still staring at the ceiling. I fold my hands over my tan tien. The center of chi. Sea of energy. I feel a stirring, a rumbling.

"I don't know what I need," I say, and in our white room, with Batman's ominous musings in the background, it sounds like the truest thing I've ever said.

The Half Penny Man

Every morning the young man, Daniel, went off to the cafe to write. As he sat in the cafe, he stared out the windows with a certain yearning at the raucous young men and women who loitered on the street corners and spilled in and out of the arcades and bars. But he was determined not to be lured from his work.

He'd found an editor, one of the tops in the city, who had agreed to pay him a half penny a word. It was a rough, hardscrabble neighborhood, and many turned to drink, gambling, petty crime, and prostitution. Some, like Daniel's father, went into plumbing, one of the few successful trades in town. Edgar, Daniel's older brother, had dutifully followed his father into the trade, but Daniel had disappointed his father by following his own dream.

When Mr. Urzik took him on, he warned Daniel, "Just don't waste your time drinking and hanging out with a loose crowd." He had seen the half penny writers come and go, and he knew that drinking and hanging out with a loose crowd led to their ruin.

"Oh no, sir, I won't," he assured Mr. Urzik.

Mr. Urzik was pleased with his progress. It was disillusioning to Daniel, though, to look out one day and spy Mr. Urzik, a plump, bearded man, normally dapper in his suit, now with his tie awry, laughing with a scantily-clad woman on the street corner. A few minutes later, Mr. Urzik straightened his tie and headed back to the editorial office, a certain spryness in his heavy legs.

Daniel spent from dawn to dusk in the cafe, developing a minor urinary infection from the quantities of coffee he consumed. Winter set in and he stared at the snow-speckled red shawls of women lingering on the corner. But he would brace himself and return to his words. He had set himself a goal of five thousand words a day, and he would work late into the evening if necessary. Once he panicked when his pencil was stolen during a bathroom break. But the culprit, an out of work half-penny writer, was found lurking over a notepad on the other side of the cafe near the fireplace. When Daniel was able to identify some distinguishing teeth marks below the eraser, it was returned unharmed.

Each night he brought his pages full of words to Mr. Urzik's office and waited nervously for his editor's reaction. "Crap, crap, sheer crap," Mr. Urzik had muttered on more than one occasion, but Daniel sensed a secret admiration hidden in the gruff voice.

Mr. Urzik sat behind his massive desk, adjusting his reading glasses, frowning. His heavy jowls and bushy moustache gave him a walrus-like appearance. He ran a stubby fingernail beneath each word, silently counting the words one by one, his lips moving, the ends of his moustache twittering as he breathed. Sometimes he backtracked, taking a second hard look at a word, and one night he gave Daniel a sharp look, his eyes glinty beneath his glasses. "Uneasy," he read from the page. "Why 'uneasy'? Can you explain why you chose that word?"

Daniel shrugged. "I'm not sure. It just came to me." He didn't know how to explain the way the words just came to him sometimes, more as if he were taking dictation than consciously choosing them.

Mr. Urzik frowned, his gaze lingering long on Daniel's earnest face. "It's a curious word for someone so young. There are many who don't get to such a word until they're much older. If they ever do. It's the sort of word..." His eyes turned soft and unfocused, as if he were searching for a memory from the distant past, but then he cleared his throat and returned to his counting. When he was done, he sat upright and let out a satisfied breath. "I count 4, 812. Not bad."

As Mr. Urzik reached in his drawer for his penny rolls, Daniel broke in, chest tight. "I'm sorry to disagree with you, sir, but I'm sure there were 5, 013. I counted them twice."

Mr. Urzik's hands froze on the desk drawer. He sat back, not blinking as he stared at Daniel. "I've been in this business a long time, young man. You don't get to where I'm at by miscounting."

"No sir. Of course not. I'm only suggesting..."

Mr. Urzik held up Daniel's pages to the light as if some fine, foul dust had fallen upon them. He leaned forward, speaking in a hushed man-to-man voice. "My boy, I'm going to let you in on a secret. Word counting isn't an exact science. You don't realize how generously I've been treating you. There are many editors who will not even pay for 'a' or 'the' or for any words referring to animals organs. We can recount if you like, but maybe I won't be so generous next time."

Daniel's throat constricted. It was a thing of honor to produce the five thousand words each day. He would have to be more careful, provide more documentation and footnotes to receive proper credit. He knew, though, that with so many writers out of work, he'd be blacklisted if he fell out with Mr. Urzik. "4, 812 will do," he mumbled out of his tight throat.

He waited while Mr. Urzik counted out 2,406 pennies, one by one. He filled his pockets with the pennies and walked to the door, but as he opened it, Mr. Urzik called from his desk, "Don't be afraid to use a bigger word now and then. Cut loose a bit."

His mother already had dinner on the table when he returned home, where he lived with his parents and older brother. His father was a bathroom builder, from the old school, and a septic odor lingered about him.

Daniel's older brother, Edgar, had followed in his father's footsteps.

"How the writing going?' his father asked at the supper table. His thick forearms were covered in white caulking.

"Not bad."

"Well, don't screw up your eyes. We can't afford glasses. No raise yet? Still a half penny a word?"

"It's the going rate," he said. "If I stick with it, it will be a penny one day."

"One day," his father said, opening his hands as if waiting for an object to fall into them.

"How many words did you write today, Shakespeare?" Edgar asked.

"5, 013. But I was only paid for 4, 812."

His father's face reddened. "Why do you put up with that?"

Daniel's mother smiled and pushed the potatoes at her husband. "I'm sure they were all very good words."

Daniel shrugged. "They were okay."

"I've seen those writers," Edgar sneered. "They're a weird bunch. I hate the way their pockets jingle."

Their father threw down his napkin. "Come on, Edgar," he said, "let's put in a water saver."

One night Daniel was invited to a fine party at Mr. Urzik's house. It was attended by writers and editors and other luminaries. There was a radical young writer there, Rad Flyer, who had made a name for himself and was no longer paid by the word but by the paragraph. Dressed foppishly, handsome, hair hanging low on his brow, he was drunk and exuberant.

"Short paragraph, long, one sentence, one word, I don't give a damn!" he roared. "It's a buck a paragraph, take it or leave it!"

Tess, his editor, sat silently, a sad smile on her face. What could she do? If she didn't pay it, someone else would. Times were changing, and she knew she was one of the old guard who would fall if she didn't adapt.

Rad did a kind of buck dance around the parlor, long hair flinging about. Mr. Urzik's lips tightened and his eyes narrowed. His walrus-like moustache quivered.

"Tess!" Rad bellowed. "Get your purse out!" Right there in the parlor, he whipped out pen and paper and dashed off not one but eleven paragraphs, some hardly more than a line long. "Pay me! Or I'll find someone who will!"

With a tight little smile, she dug in her purse and counted out eleven one dollar bills.

"Hah!" Rad cried triumphantly. "Let's get drunk, boys!"

He grabbed at the other writers, pulling and pushing them toward the door.

"I can't go. I need my sleep to be fresh in the morning," Daniel demurred, catching sight of Mr. Urzik's glowering mien.

"Come on, buddy boy." Rad tugged at his sleeve. "You're the one I want to talk to. You're the only reason I came to this awful party." He headlocked the resisting Daniel and dragged him out the door, calling back with a defiant roar, "Screw all you editors!" With that, he led the writers into the street.

The next evening, as always, Daniel brought his words to Mr. Urzik's office. There were 5,004 exactly. He had counted them three times.

Mr. Urzik did not look up at Daniel as he counted. He ran his blunt fingertip below each word, his nostrils narrowing and opening as he breathed. His finger paused below a word. *"Elongated.* Where did that wretched word come from? From Mr. Flyer?"

Before Daniel could answer, Mr. Urzik wagged his head and shoulders mockingly. "I know. It just *came* to you. 'Elongated' indeed. You should be ashamed of yourself." Mr. Urzik walked to the window and looked down at the snowy street. When he turned back, Daniel noticed for the first time the threadbare elbows of Mr. Urzik's suit. "You think you're on to something with your clever words like 'elongated', but you're going in the wrong direction. Desk. Book. Armchair. Water. Caulk. Those are good words. 'Secretly' is a little disturbing, but understandable. Down river? I can't tell whether you mean that as one or two words. I've a good mind to dock you on that."

"I thought you wanted me to cut loose."

Mr. Urzik loomed over his desk, gripping the edges. "A *bit,* young man. But this is *anarchy.* And so help me, if I ever see you use that word..." He'd gotten out of breath. He rubbed at his flabby, sweaty neck. "But there's more to it, isn't there?"

Daniel could not meet Mr. Urzik's fierce eyes. They were much like his father's on the day Daniel had told him he wasn't going into the family business.

"Oh yes," Mr. Urzik said. "There's *more,* isn't there, Daniel? You've got big thoughts now, haven't you? Mr. Flyer has filled you with his ideas. *Paragraph* writer! And where does it end? He'll fill your head with all sorts of twisted notions. Paragraphs? That won't hold you for long. A paragraph will be too good for the likes of you. A story. That's what. You'll want to be paid by the *story.* And how much will you want then?"

"Thirty dollars," Daniel mumbled. He slid his chair back to avoid a thrust of the desk against his diaphragm.

Mr. Urzik staggered from the desk. A stronger timbre came to Daniel's voice as he spoke to the rotund figure who looked poised to hurl himself from the window. "That's right. I want thirty dollars a story from now on. Long, short, a short short, I don't care. Thirty dollars. That's my price."

Mr. Urzik wiggled his fingers in the air as if besieged by invisible flying insects. "That's his price, long, short, short short, it doesn't matter, that's his price." He pressed his face to the glass and breathed until a halo of mist spread over the pane. He sank back in his chair and talked quietly, as a doctor to a patient who has failed to follow orders and will now die. "You were an upcoming word man. They were nice words you chose. I was willing to forgive you when you slipped up now and then." He lifted one of Daniel's old pages and read fondly from it: "Coffee, desk, saucer...Those are good words. 'Urination' is a little tougher, but I can live with it. I wouldn't use it in certain crowds."

He set the page down. "I will never pay for stories. I buy words. A half penny a word. As if that's nothing?" He held up a beefy hand. "I know that things change. In my father's time, the writers worked underground. They were never let out. That was wrong, we know that now. But now, many live among us almost normally. I'm for change. But slowly. A little more slowly please. This talk of paragraphs, and now *story* writing? Where will it lead?" His eyes closed. "I'm too old for it. I'm just not ready."

His eyes opened and he looked at Daniel. "Sit while I recount. I think you counted an adjective twice on the second page."

As Mr. Urzik silently recounted the words, Daniel sat listening to his own heartbeat. The night before with Rad came back to him. They'd been drunk in that wild way where visions are born and they had ended up beneath a bridge on the bank of an icy river, just the two of them, the other writers having drifted off with a loose crowd. The other writers were all talk and bluff. He knew they'd be back begging for their jobs once they sobered up.

There were tears in Rad's eyes. "I know you've got it, kid. I can tell." He swigged from his bottle. "I've only got so many paragraphs left in me. A whole story? Who am I kidding? I've got old Tess worried, but I don't have a story in me. I've seen you in that cafe day after day. I used to watch you through the glass. You were so intense you never noticed me." He slipped an arm around Daniel's shoulders. "One day when you were in the bathroom, I went to your table and read some of your words. One of them comes back to me as clearly as if I'm seeing it for the first time. 'Toothless.' It shook me to the bone. I left there reeling. I was drunk for two weeks."

Tears ran down Rad's face. "I wrote a great paragraph once. You can still find it in Town Hall. People spoke of me. But I used up the gift. Tess indulges me, she thinks that one day, if I ever get sober..."

He gave a sudden giddy laugh. "We'll see about *that!*" He took off his scarf and threw it down on the bank. He moved to the edge of the swift-flowing cold river.

"Hey," Daniel said. "What are you...?"

Rad dove into the water. He whooped with laughter from the rush of cold. Daniel raced along the bank as Rad rode the current, shouting out, "Tell the bastards it's thirty bucks a story from now on!" Daniel followed him through several bends in the river, but finally lost him as the river narrowed and led through a darkened woods.

Daniel rose from his chair in Mr. Urzik's office. He walked to the door as Mr. Urzik's eyes speared him in the back.

"Touch that doorknob," Mr. Urzik said. "Touch it and you can never turn back. There won't be a second chance."

Hand trembling, he touched the doorknob.

"A penny a word then," Mr. Urzik said. "It will ruin us all, but you've forced me to it."

With a penny a word, he could buy new pencils and almost all the coffee he'd ever want. He thought of what his father would say if he turned it down. He half-turned back to Mr. Urzik, then he ran down the stairs as Mr. Urzik's shout followed him. "You fool! You'll be back!"

He ran until he came to the riverbank. He looked at the dark waters and shivered. Maybe Rad was swept all the way to the next town. Even now he was working on a new paragraph, the best paragraph he'd ever written, the best paragraph ever.

His swift steps bore him back into town. It was quitting time for most and the loose crowds were gathering on the street corners, but there were still a few who labored on. He spied his father and Edgar humping down the street with sinks and plumbing fixtures on their backs. He retreated into the shadows.

He sat at the table he had always used, but it felt different tonight. Glancing through the window, he spotted Tess standing beneath a street lamp, sniffling, looking lost. He suddenly realized she was staring back at him. He lifted his pencil in hello. She straightened her spine, stuffed her tissues back in her purse and headed across the street with a determined stride. Well, let her talk. He knew his price.

The Murderer

The murderer held a gun to my temple. He must have noticed the troubled expression on my face because he sighed and inquired, "What's wrong now?"

"Feel here," I said. "Here on the side of my head, just below the barrel of the gun."

The blunt chubby fingers of his free hand searched my hair just above my ear. "I don't feel anything."

"More to the right." I guided his fingers with mine. His touch was awkward. He would have made a poor doctor or barber.

He sighed again. He was a plump man, red-faced and sweaty, easily put out by things, though he had a pleasant way of dressing, a checkered wool shirt and crisp khaki pants that gave him a gentrified country air. He had captured me in town and led me into the woods to murder me. The woods were aflame with red and gold colors, the foliage wet and glistening after a morning shower.

"So what's wrong with your head?" he asked.

"I've got some sort of lump."

"I still don't feel-Oh! There."

"You feel it now?"

"I think I do. What is it?"

"Well, I was worried it might be cancer."

"*Cancer!*" he scoffed. "Don't be ridiculous. You worry too much."

"You don't think it is?"

"Of course not." He frowned, felt the lump again. "How long have you had it?"

"A few months."

"A few *months?* Did you see anyone?"

"No. I felt silly. I was afraid it was nothing."

He lowered his gun and tucked it into his waistband. "Look, you can't play around with stuff like that. You can't just be letting things grow on your head. Okay? I mean something grows on your head, you get it checked for Christ's sake."

He sighed. "Well, I guess we should get this over with." He took his gun back out. "Turn around."

He put the gun to the back of my head. He was gentle with the pressure, for a clumsy sort.

I sighed. I made a little sound in my throat.

"What now?"

"I was just feeling a little sad."

"*Sad?* Why? Why on earth are you feeling sad?"

"Oh. It's nothing. I just feel full of memories, when the children were small, my wife's passing away. Sometimes I can see myself as a boy of three or four...So innocent, full of life...Then we grow up...Life does things to us."

"Please," he said. "Let's not start getting heavy, shall we? Damn!" he muttered.

"What?"

"You've made me sad now. All that talk."

"Sorry."

"Forget it." He sank his thick haunches down on a rock. I joined him. The barrel of the gun dangled down toward the mud at our feet.

"I'm not going to cry," he said.

Then his shoulders shook and he held a hand to his face.

'I'm sorry," I said.

"No," he said. "It's not you. This is very inappropriate of me. Here." He handed me the gun. "Just kill me," he said.

I held the barrel to his head as he shut his eyes tight. Then I tried the ribcage. Nothing felt right. "I can't do it," I said.

51

"No. No, of course not." He eased the gun from my hand.

"Well, if you really insist."

"No. No, that was my moment of softness. That was it."

He was businesslike now. He stood up. "Time to murder you now."

He pressed the gun to the back of my head, and when he drew in a breath, I ran. "Hey, come back here, knock it off!" he shouted. He fired at me, but I ran in a zigzag, and the bullets whacked into the mud. I bolted through the trees, running like a young man again, jumping over fallen logs. The woods were so wet and alive and I could hear him calling behind me, but I was in better shape and I ran and his voice fell away into the distance until there was only the tiniest whisper in my ear: Time to murder you, time to murder you, time to murder you…

Teach Us

Show us some things, we ask our new teacher.
We sit in the floor in a circle, looking at him as he
stands, surrounded by us.

We are young, though not children. He is older,
but not old, though a look crosses his face as if he is
tired, as if he has seen things he wishes he had not seen.

He doesn't really want to teach us. His eyes
slide to the metal door as if he's measuring the steps,
calculating how quickly he can escape.

I don't know that I really have anything to show
you, he says.

But we heard that you were good. You won
tournaments.

To tell the truth, he says, that was mostly a
myth. I had a good day now and then. Once or twice I
was lucky. But that was a long time ago.

Why have you come here, then?

For the money, he says, though it's not much.
But I suppose I can't expect better at this point.

Still, we say, you're here. Show us something.
Show us the one-finger push.

The one-finger push, he says, yes, well, it would
probably work on most of you. You don't look so
tough, but what about him? The big fellow?

The big fellow grins and rises to his feet. His
biceps bulge from his T-shirt. Below his gray shorts,
his huge calf muscles twitch. He played linebacker in
college. He has the shifty eyes of one accustomed to
being attacked from several directions at once. He
grins. Sure, push me.

The teacher sighs. He is not large. There's a bit
too much pot to his belly. You are very strong, he says,
I don't know if this will work on you.

Come on, the big fellow, the linebacker, says.

The teacher touches his index finger to the center of the linebacker's chest. The linebacker grins, but the lines tighten around his eyes.

The teacher gives a small, almost imperceptible push with his finger. The linebacker goes nowhere. If anything, his feet seem to sink deeper into the floor. Hah! he snorts. He swells up with blood and muscle. He looks like he could charge and drive the teacher into the wall, shatter his spine and the back of his head. It looks hopeless for the teacher. We feel bad for him, but we are angry, too. Why did he come here when we are already in such despair? What does he know of our troubles? He may feel trapped like us, but at the end of the day he will be free to leave.

The teacher frowns. You're even bigger than I thought, he says.

Come on, the linebacker says, take another shot.

He frowns. He shrugs his shoulders. He pushes again and the linebacker steps back.

The teacher's shoulders sink pleasurably as if he's just been massaged. Step in here again, he says to the linebacker.

The linebacker steps back in, and again the teacher springs him back with a little push of his finger. The big fellow stops grinning; he grimaces, his face turns red. Time and again the teacher lightly pushes and makes him step back.

Sweat pours down the linebacker's face. The veins beat in his temples. The cords stand out on his thick neck. He sinks into a ballplayer's stance, one fist apelike on the ground, the other arm across his massive thigh. His calf muscles throb. He crouches on his toes, ready to burst through the line and sack the quarterback. The teacher makes a small sound in his throat, it might be a chuckle, and he touches the side of the linebacker's shoulder and thrusts him to the floor.

The linebacker bounces up grinning. He tries to pull grass from his teeth, though there is no grass in this windowless room. The linebacker's eyes travel into the past, into packed cheering stadiums. He travels into bright chilly afternoons, his jersey stained with blood, his breath in puffs of fog between the bars of his face guard. Travels into bright, chilly afternoons, the scent of smoke and dying autumn in the air.

Hah! he snaps, this guy's great!

But already the teacher's shoulders are drawing in, and the light fades from his eyes. He shrugs.

Can you teach us that?

No.

Why not?

I don't know how to teach it. I could line you up and demonstrate it again and again, and we would get nowhere. I could have you practice it repeatedly, and it would not work. You all seem a little slow to me. I'm not complaining. If I were you, I would go to another teacher, if possible. There are young people who know how to explain it. It seems mostly a matter of luck to me. Sometimes I'm lucky. I could be humiliated a minute from now. You could push me right over.

Could we try? we ask.

He sighs. All right, then, if you must.

One by one we charge him. Sometimes he stands there like an oak, letting us push on him until we fall exhausted to the floor. Other times he turns his waist like a matador, and we go stumbling past him. Finally we all wade in on him at once, and he spins about, his arms moving like great windmills, and he whirls us into the corners and walls.

Teach us, teach us please, we cry eagerly. How do you do it?

Luck, he whispers almost with hatred. I don't know. He stares fiercely at us. Let me be.

We sink back down on the floor in our circle, lost in our despair. The linebacker's eyes glaze over. He is running off the field while the cheerleaders jump on the sidelines. He glimpses the red of their panties as their skirts flip up on their magnificent legs. They cheer: Big fellow! Big fellow! Big fellow! as they wave their pom-poms. The linebacker sits with us now, both knees all zippered with stitches.

I'll be here once a week, the teacher says. That's all I can do.

We look up at him. Our eyes widen. You'll teach us?

I'll be here.

You'll show us the one-finger push?

I'll be here, he says.

We look at each other. Something loosens in our chests. The linebacker slaps his palms on his great thighs. Whoo-hoo! he chortles. Here we go!

The teacher turns. Next week, he calls over his shoulder. He leaves us there as the guard lets him out. We sit, shoulders bumping together, a clock ticking in the silence.

Silence

After our showers, towels draped around our waists, our freshman football team assembled in the locker room at St. John's High. We'd just finished our last practice before the first game of the season. We'd toughened beneath the sweltering south Texas sun, learned to take a hit and bounce up grinning.

Coach Baker, a short man with a bristling crew cut, stood before the coach's cage in his customary long gray shorts, a heavy set of keys suspended on his belt. He crossed his muscular arms over his chest and frowned at us. His son, Kevin, my best friend, breathed wheezily beside me.

Coach Meyers, the assistant, joined Coach Baker, standing behind a metal folding chair and resting his jutting T-shirted belly against it. He was tremendously overweight but very strong. He reminded us of the great Russian weightlifters.

"Boys," Coach Baker said. His gruff voice reverberated off the concrete floor and high, metal-girded ceiling. "When we started practice a few weeks ago, I was disgusted. I saw things that sickened my stomach." Coach Meyers wagged his enormous head; he, too, had been sickened. "But I'm proud of you now. You've come a long way." His frown intensified. "But we still don't have a prayer against Holy Cross." Coach Meyers whistled through his teeth.

Though we wouldn't play Holy Cross until the last game of the season, for weeks the coaches had alarmed us with tales of freshmen just released from the state reformatory. In pile-ups, they would jab their fingers up our nostrils and gouge our eyes with their thumbs.

"To win this year, we can't play like a bunch of hotshots. We've got to play like a *team!* We've got to *look* like a team, not a bunch of damn hippies." He stroked his crew cut. "*This* is a haircut for football players."

Nimble on his fat legs, Coach Meyers ducked into the coach's cage and carried out an electric hair clippers trailed by a bright orange extension cord, and we collectively gasped. It was 1968, and most of us wore our hair like the Beatles. Clustered in our bare feet, still damp from the showers, we muttered in protest, but Coach Baker glared us into silence.

Our only hope was Kevin, who sometimes could temper his father's excesses and rages. Kevin was slight, asthmatic, but a gutsy receiver who'd leap for catches and take fierce hits in the back. "People will laugh, Dad," Kevin said.

His father's eyes glittered with contempt. "It's not *'Dad'* in this locker room! It's *Coach.* The same as everybody else! There are no hotshots on this team!"

Kevin lowered his eyes. "Yes sir."

Coach Baker's voice turned husky. "There's a war going on, boys. Some of you might end up in it. The athletes survive because they stick together. The hotshots don't make it, do they, Coach Meyers?"

"No, they don't, Coach. They sure don't."

Coach Baker pointed a finger at Kevin. "You're first."

As Kevin sat in the metal chair, his eyes went dull as his father twisted his chin. The clippers exuded a hot oily smell, and Coach Meyers looked on, lips pursed, as if he were examining the work of a master hairstylist. Coach Baker made jerky passes over Kevin's skull, and dark locks of hair fell down on Kevin's skinny chest and towel-draped lap. Coach Baker reduced Kevin's hair to stubble, then pushed him from the chair. "Who's next?"

His eyes sought mine, but I stayed frozen in place as he watched me, taking stock of my reaction.

I had seen that look on a summer morning a year before. Coach Baker had taken Kevin and me and a couple of other boys on a camping trip. The night was too warm to sleep inside the tent, so we spread our sleeping bags on the ground outside. In the night, I woke to find Coach Baker pressed against me. His scratchy cheek rubbed against mine and I felt his breath in my ear. Then I became aware of his hand inside my underwear as he slid it up and down my penis. His behavior seemed so strange to me, so out of the norm, that at first I thought I must be imagining things, or I wondered if he had been sleepwalking and in a moment he would wake in embarrassment. My heart beat fast, and I kept my eyes shut and lay as still as possible, hearing my own quick shallow breaths, trying to sink my body deeper into the ground, praying that this moment wasn't really happening. Later he melted away, slipping back into the darkness.

In the morning, he was already flipping pancakes when we rose. We kicked our way out of our sleeping bags and stumbled for the fire pit. "You ready for a pancake, Paul?" He held out a paper plate with a cake already buttered. His eyes studied me, and I silently took the plate.

He found other opportunities after that, and during the next year, he never acted as if anything strange was going on. I have fleeting memories of a hand quickly, efficiently unzipping my blue jeans and snaking inside. In one shadowy memory, we are sitting on a couch in his living room, both of us with our shorts down around our knees while he touches my penis and explains its anatomy, as if he's giving a school lesson, as if this is a perfectly normal thing to do.

I'd grown up with Kevin around the block, and because my father was away on business so often, I was often included in his family's outings, and it was Coach Baker, not my father, who had taught me how to play football and baseball. We'd always been friends I had thought. He left me out of the fierce tirades he directed at Kevin and Kevin's older brother, Doug.

Before the season began, I had resolved that he would not touch me anymore. I never said anything, but I avoided being alone with him, and he seemed offended, as if I'd betrayed him.

"Who's next?" he shouted again, watching me.

Fortunately, one of the other boys moved past me. Coach Baker handed over the clippers to Coach Meyers and disappeared inside the cage. Coach Meyers joked about opening a barber shop, and our moods lifted and we laughed and cheered each other on as one by one we lost our hair. When I took my place on the metal chair, Coach Baker came out of the cage and took the clippers back. His fingers dug into my cheeks as he angled my head. I caught sight of Kevin, and his look from the recesses of the locker room was almost prayerful, asking me for forgiveness. I prayed, too. Lord, I prayed, let the man die. Let him die, let him die, let him die.

In the week after the haircuts, jeers greeted us at school. In the corridors, palms came from behind and impersonated airplane take-offs down my flattened runway. Mirrors brought tears to my eyes. Several times, my mother remarked on how handsome I looked, but teenagers seldom appreciate such motherly niceties. I massaged the roots, coaxed the seedlings along, tugged at the ends. By mid-October, one patch in the middle had rallied, created a hillock.

Our haircuts did not propel us toward a glorious season. We'd win one week, lose the next. After each loss, Coach Baker forced us to run wind sprints directly after the games. At practices, though, by the beginning of November, he had become aloof, letting Coach Meyers run the practices. Kevin said he was preoccupied with Doug, Kevin's older brother, who was running wild while he waited to be drafted.

Left in charge, Coach Meyers humored us. After I'd made a dust-churning one-yard run, he remarked, "Paul, you may be small, but you're slow, too."

Coach Baker stood absently on the sidelines, but sometimes he'd trot across the field, a set of keys jingling on his gray shorts, stitched-knees pumping. He'd grab someone's facemask and scream at him.

As a sandlot football player in pick-up games, I'd run with pinball-like glee, bouncing off tacklers and bounding off in new directions. What joy I had felt on autumn afternoons, the smell of grass high in my nostrils as I spun through the arms encircling my thighs. But the pads weighed me down, turned me sluggish and awkward, and I could not hit the right holes or follow the blockers. From running back, I was switched to defensive safety, where I patrolled the field like a lonely scout, the plays usually over by the time I arrived on the scene.

Coach Baker watched me from the sidelines, and in the locker room, and whenever we passed in the school corridors.

Late autumn turned chilly and gray. My father was often away on his sales trips, and a space had widened between Kevin and me. I shuffled down busy corridors but seemed always alone in the crowd. I sat quietly in classrooms, avoiding the horseplay, studying the teachers. Was there one I could trust? On afternoon, in the darkness of a confessional in the chapel, I whispered through a screen to kindly old Father Finley, "I let a man...touch me."

I heard his soft breathing, the shift of his rosary beads in his lap, and he muttered sadly, "Oh, my son.

This is weighing on you. Someone has hurt you badly."
I could sense he was trying to identify my voice, and I
ran from the confessional, ran from the empty chapel as
his confessional door opened and he called to my
fleeing back. But in a moment, I was through the door
to the outside, running down the hill, disappearing.

One Saturday night, I snuck a pint of bourbon
from my parents' liquor cabinet and brought it to a
school dance, where the liquor provided a passport for
Kevin and me to drink with the older boys in the
bleachers beside the track and football field. "Drink," I
said, holding the pint to Kevin's mouth, but he made a
face and spat it out. I didn't spit mine out. The elixir
flowed through my veins, melted the chill inside. I
laughed, I shouted. The older boys told me to shut up,
but my voice came spewing up and I cursed at them and
called them names. They dragged me out of the
bleachers, laughing as they threw me to the ground.
But I rose up, relentless. A junior on the bottom
bleacher had his arm around a pretty blonde girl. I held
out my hand. "Marry me," I said. Her lovely teeth
sparkled in the night before the junior and his friends
jumped me.
As they pummeled me, I bolted across the track
to the field. Shouting, the older boys gave chase. The
field was alive with moving shadows, but with no pads
to weigh me down, I dodged and darted until Kevin was
running beside me, calling, "Come on! Over the
fence!" We leapt the fence and ran into the woods until
the shouting of our pursuers fell away behind us.
"You idiot," Kevin said as we went deeper into
the woods.
"I'm not afraid of them," I said. "I'm going
back for that woman."
He tripped me, knelt over me and pinned me to
the ground. "What's wrong with you?"

"I've got to tell you something about your father. Something he did to me."

His hand clamped my mouth and he hissed, "Shut up! You're drunk!" He punched my face, then he lifted a rock from the ground and held it over my head and sobbed, "Shut up! Shut up!"

At Kevin's house, in a far corner of the yard, stood a dilapidated, tiny guesthouse. Over the years, the guesthouse had served various purposes. It had been our clubhouse once, and for a while Kevin's mother had made it into an office space. At other times, it merely housed tools and supplies. But in recent weeks, Kevin's father had banished Kevin's older brother Doug from the main house and exiled him in the little house. He was not even permitted into the main house for meals, and Kevin's father had ordered Kevin to stay away from him.

One chilly night in early December, Kevin and I pitched a tent in the back yard, hidden from the main house by a grove of trees. We sat at the front flap of the tent, telling stories, when we saw shadowy figures move across the lawn. Then lights came on in the little house.

We crept across the yard and tapped on the door. The door cracked open, and Doug's strong hands reached out and dragged us in. He breathed boozily on us. "What do you want?"

He pushed us toward a ratty throw rug on the floor, and he sank back down on a rickety bed. At the foot of the bed slouched a friend of his, Kyle, a tall, skinny kid who wore his red hair in an Afro. He was dressed in an oversized navy surplus P-jacket, and his buck teeth and purple acne made him impressively ugly. He leaned over and rapped his sharp knuckles on my skull. "Drill a hole there," he said, "and you'd look just like my ass."

Doug was muscular like his father, and with his curly dark hair and rugged face, he cut a romantic figure as he lounged on the bed, back against the wall. In a thick self-mocking voice, he told us he'd received his draft notice that afternoon. "I'm going to get killed anyway. So first patrol out, I run into the jungle firing my rifle. Those fuckers will have to kill me clean."

Kevin rocked forward from his cross-legged position, his arms wrapped around his knees. "Don't go, Doug. Run away."

Doug shrugged. "I'm the kind of guy they want, little brother. I'm just meat on the fucking hoof."

Kyle sneered. "Fuck Vietnam. I've got my own war here. I killed two narcs yesterday."

Kevin and I stiffened in shock, but Doug shook his head to signal that Kyle was lying. "The narcs are okay. They're just doing their jobs." He aimed his finger at Kyle's chest. "I'll tell you this. I'm glad we live in a country where they try to put people like you and me away."

From the depths of his furry naval jacket, Kyle produced a cellophane baggie full of brown-green leaves. Spreading a record album over his lap, he laid out rolling papers. His yellow tongue licked at the glue to join the papers. Gnarly, corroded-looking fingertips dipped into the baggie and dropped a pinch of the leaves between the papers. I had never seen marijuana before, but I knew this must be the very stuff.

"Put that shit away around these guys," Doug said.

"They got to learn sometime," Kyle said. "You don't want them to learn from amateurs, do you?" He twisted the ends of the joint, and his tongue licked again, sealing the seam. "Let's get these cherries stoned and paint their balls yellow."

64

"Put it away, Kyle. I know you're scum and I can accept that, but you don't have to be a fucking hotshot around these guys."

"Fucking cherries," Kyle muttered. He slipped the baggie back into his cavernous jacket, but he held the rolled joint in his palm, proffering it like a jewel to the heathens. "This is fucking *gold,*" he said reverently. "You want me to put fucking gold away? Has the army already fucked up your mind?"

"Let's go," Kevin said.

He started to rise, but I pulled him back down. Quiet descended over us. The bottom limbs of an old oak tree scratched against the windowpanes as we sat in the thick silence of criminals. Kyle produced a lighter. He inhaled like a man drawing his last gasp of air. As a pungent odor filled the cramped room, his eyes widened and he clutched one hand to his chest as the other hand made a stiff sidearm handoff to Doug. "Holy *shit,*" Kyle squeaked. "I can't even, I can't even..." He waggled both hands in the air as tears flooded his eyes.

Doug took a measured hit, tilting his chin and contemplating the ceiling through the drifting smoke. When he lowered his eyes, he looked at Kevin alone. His voice came out husky. "This stuff can be okay. If you use it right." He hovered over us like a shadowy brooding angel. "Never take advantage of anyone. Don't be selfish with your weed. Never cut it with tobacco." With a graceful swoop of his hand, Doug turned the butt end toward Kevin's lips, and Kevin's hand tremulously lifted to take the smoking joint.

The wind had picked up and there was a creaking and pushing sound at the door. Kyle cried, "Narcs! Eat the pot!"

Kevin's father burst in like a commando. "Throw it on the floor!" he screamed. Kevin dropped the burning joint on the throw rug, and I jumped up and tramped it with my foot.

Kyle made a shrieking sound and sprung through the door into the night. Kevin's father let him go, but he thrust Kevin and me aside, grabbed Doug's throat and shoved him down on the bed, kneeling over him as he banged Doug's head up and down on the mattress and screamed, *"Give dope to your little brother! I ought to choke the life out of you!"*

"Go ahead," Doug gritted.

His father delivered a flurry of open-handed slaps to Doug's face. Kevin came from behind and grabbed at his father's arms. His father backhanded him and Kevin reeled into me. Blood spurted from his nose. He dove back at his father, trying to hold his arms. "Dad!" he screamed. "Doug got drafted!"

The hail of blows slowed and then stopped. Coach Baker panted for air. He knelt over Doug, who lay in near silence, only a sniffling sound coming from his nose. Kevin was sobbing, laying his body over his father's broad back. Coach Baker pushed him off and stood in the middle of the room, eyes rolling from Kevin to Doug to me. He hugged his arms about himself, looking as if he were in the midst of strangers. Kevin was wheezing, and he pulled his asthma inhalator from his jeans pocket. Doug sat up, his mouth bloody.

In a deadened voice, Coach Baker said to him, "I want you to clear out of here." Then his eyes bore in on me as I cowered in the doorway. "You led Kevin on to this." He stepped toward me, but Kevin blocked his path and yelled, "Run!"

As I broke into the darkness, Coach Baker's enraged voice carried after me. "You're no better than us!"

His voice seemed to follow me as I ran down alleyways, and it was still with me as I let myself through the back door into my own quiet home. As usual when my father was away, my mother was sitting up late in the den, with only the soft blue light of the T.V. In her nightgown, she adjusted her legs so I could join her on the couch.

"I thought you were staying over at Kevin's."

"It got too cold in the tent."

"I'll make some popcorn." She sniffed. "You've been smoking."

"We tried a cigarette. We didn't like it."

She sighed. "Don't get started, honey. It's hell to quit."

The television cast a comforting pool of light as we watched a western starring Jimmy Stewart. Tall, gaunt, and benign, Jimmy Stewart looked as if he might understand any secret one might tell him.

I was an only child, and in the absence of my father, my mother and I were comfortable companions, but it was a quiet friendship consisting of order and routine and simple offerings: I'll make popcorn, honey...I'll take the trash out, Mom...I had no clue of how to speak of Coach Baker, no way of knowing how to explain the times I had frozen and surrendered.

I stayed on the couch by her side, and when the movie was over I asked her to stay up and watch another show with me.

Memory throws an image on the screen: It is twilight in late autumn, and a boy wanders out to a lone oak tree on the hill behind the school. The boy looks westward, and the dying sunset casts a reddish glow on the horizon. The boy pulls up the collar of his coat, sinks his hands into his pants pockets. He stares past tennis courts, past the tarp-covered school pool, and up a hill of mesquite trees towards the girls' parochial school. Somewhere the boy's father is out driving the state highways, and he wishes himself into his father's car, pictures himself on the leather seat beside his father while the black nose of the sedan guides them smoothly past the glinting, brackish backwaters of the Gulf of Mexico. The boy opens his mouth to speak, but his father plunges the accelerator down and the car leaps and goes faster. The tires hum to a fine high pitch and the brackish waters glide by, darkening. I have something to tell you, the boy says, and his father's face forms a frozen smile as he stares straight ahead at the road. The boy sinks back in the leather seat, and settles deeper into the silence.

The Friday afternoon after the fiasco at Kevin's, we played our last game against Holy Cross. All that week at practice, Coach Baker had averted his eyes from me. Kevin had told me that Doug had moved out, and that his father had hardly spoken all week.

The Holy Cross team was formidable, but their offense primarily consisted of their quarterback, a tall lanky kid who found receivers at will. When he limped off the field in the third quarter and was replaced by a second-stringer, we made a comeback and tied the game.

The possibility of beating Holy Cross whipped Coach Baker into a frenzy. He screamed and trotted along the sidelines, and when he sent in subs, he practically flung them onto the field.

But with two minutes to go, their first-string quarterback limped back on the field. When he took the snaps and backpedaled to throw, his knee nearly buckled, but still he marched his team down the field with short, perfect passes. Coach Baker called timeout and gathered our defense on the sidelines. "We've got to stop that quarterback," he said.

He stared long at me and called for me to make a safety blitz. "Come at him hard," he said. Coach

Meyers listened from the perimeter of the huddle, and an uneasy expression flitted across his face.

As I trotted back on the field, I realized Coach Baker was making me an offer to come back into his good graces. And what is absolutely insane is how desperately I wanted to be back in his good graces, how desperately I wanted his approval.

I edged closer, and on the snap I charged through a sieve in the line. Running at full tilt, I sighted in on the quarterback, lowered my helmet and drove into his bad knee. We fell in a tangle and players from both teams threw themselves into the pile-up, and when the pile-up cleared, I stood back and watched the quarterback writhe in agony on the cold turf.

When I trotted from the field, Coach Baker patted my helmet. I caught Coach Meyers' eye for a moment before he turned his vast shoulders from me.

As the boy lay on the field, the coaches from the other team hovered over him. Parents on the other sidelines yelled at us, and parents on our sideline yelled back. People from both sides infiltrated the field and started yelling and pushing. The ref blew his whistle and pronounced the game over. As the fans of the other team jeered us, I carried my helmet on my last walk to the locker room.

I can't say now what compelled me to do so, but in the summer, I went with the Bakers on a fishing trip. My only real memory of the trip consists of this: Coach Baker and I are on the outboard together as it lolls in the lake, just the two of us, fishing and smoking cigars. I'm getting woozy from the cigar and the slow roll of the boat. He swims in and out of my vision as he sits in the stern of the boat, one hand holding his fishing rod, his other hand holding the tiller. "You may not believe this," he says. "But I am your friend."

I don't say anything, but I look away toward shore, to the tiny dots of figures on the land. My head wobbles. I must have a certain expression on my face because he says, "Why do you look that way when I say that? You are my friend."

There's a haze between us, a blur. "Okay?" he says. The land seems far away and I am on the boat alone with him, and I watch his hand on the tiller as if he's thinking of steering us farther from shore. With his legs, he makes the small boat rock a little more from side to side. "Okay," I say.

"Okay? We're okay?"

"Let's go back," I say. "I'm sick."

He looks at me.

"The cigar."

He makes a little chuckling sound, and he turns the boat toward shore. I close my eyes and the motion of the boat vibrates through me as we buck over the little waves of the lake.

The Bike

Henderson heard the automatic garage door opening and he came out to greet Janet. Her new job selling real estate meant longer evenings away, and her late arrivals didn't fit in with his vision of things—a cheery little supper, and over the meal an exchange of work stories revealing small moments of triumph and disappointment. But since she'd started the real estate job, by the time she arrived home, they were both tired.

This evening, though, she hopped out of her Honda, smiled brightly at him and moved to the back of her car, opening her hand like a game show hostess displaying a prize, a shiny new red mountain bike mounted on a rack. He did not pay attention to the bike at first, but to the rack, which he recognized. They'd had the rack even before they were married, but he thought it had disappeared, parted with at a garage sale, along with the aging road bikes they'd quit riding years ago.

"Where'd you find that old thing?" he asked.

"I just dug around."

"*When?* I didn't notice you looking for anything."

She wore a flushed grinning look and touched the front tire of the bike. "Do you like it?"

He stopped frowning at the rack and studied the bike. "What are you going to do with it?"

She rolled her eyes and made a swishing of air sound. "Well, if you don't know what you do with a bike..."

"No. No, I mean...Do you want some help?"

"I can do it."

As Janet untied the straps, she positioned her sturdy shoulders between him and the handlebars, which he wanted to ease from her. He pictured disasters, flights through the air, her pretty chin striking the pavement. "Couldn't you just ride an exercise bike at the gym?"

As she lifted the bike from the rack, he reached a hand past her, touching the rear tire in an effort to help, but succeeding only in getting in the way, and as she swung the bike around, he backed off.

She propped the bike against the car and patted the hard black seat. "What do you think?"

"I didn't know you wanted another bike."

"I mentioned it a lot of times."

"You did?"

She opened the back door of the car and came out with a helmet in her hand. She pulled it over her head, working it over her long full hair, which was still blonde except for some graying around her ears. She snapped the strap around her chin, wincing as the strap pinched her. Her blonde hair streaming out from beneath the helmet gave her a Viking demeanor. "You could get a bike, too, you know."

He shrugged. "You're not going to ride now? In the dark?"

She patted him on the chest. "Just once around the block."

She rolled the bike away from the car and swung one leg over the seat. In her slacks and flat shoes, she moved gracefully, as if it hadn't been years since she'd ridden.

Her headlight cast a thin beam into the darkness as she rode down the steep driveway, and she hardly seemed to check left or right as she wheeled into the suburban street. Theirs was a quiet neighborhood of shady streets and light traffic, but it still did not feel right to have her riding off alone into the darkness. He stood in the driveway, looking after her, calling out too late for her to hear, "Be careful!"

Later, he would hear her words in his mind: *You could get a bike, too.* What if he'd said, "Okay, sure, I'll get a bike." Maybe he could have turned it all around right there. He could see them in his mind, the way it might have been—the two of them riding down a country lane, riding through a rain of autumn leaves, side by side, smiles of rapture on their faces. But he suspected that the image wasn't original, that he might have stolen it from anti-depressant commercials. Sometimes in the images, they were joined by Joshua, whom they'd lost ten years before when he was nine, drowned when he was off camping with another child's parents. Both he and the other boy had slipped from the bank into a swiftly moving river. No one had seen them fall, and Henderson would wonder later if Joshua had tried to rescue the other boy, and he supposed maybe the other parents wondered if their child had tried to rescue Joshua. When the images of Joshua on the bike came to him, he allowed them for a few moments, to relish Joshua again, to celebrate the perky, smiling boy he had been, but the images left him so terribly shaken that he fled from them by working in the garden, shoveling and turning soil until his legs felt weak.

Why, though, had it seemed so impossible, too late to say: *Yes, I'll get a bike. I'll ride with you.*

But if he'd said yes, would she have really been happy? Would they have ridden a few times, and then have stored the bikes in a far corner of the garage, left the bikes to rust, more years gliding by until one day the bikes were back out in the driveway along with some boxes of books and old sweaters? Some kid would beam at one of the bikes and his Dad would offer ten dollars, and then someone else would take the other, and later he and Janet would walk back inside from the garage sale, his hand on her elbow.

Maybe he'd done her a favor by not joining her on her rides. He would have slowed her down. There'd be roads he wouldn't want to take. He'd worry about the weather and what to wear and where would they stop to eat. Were they spending too much time? Wasn't there something else he should be doing? Shouldn't he be grading papers or planning class or doing some terribly important things like preparing dinner or paying bills or checking the email or watering the lawn? Weren't there lots of important things he should be doing instead of riding on glorious country lanes with the leaves blowing around his ears?

It was never really a true image for him that they could have ridden off together into sunrises and sunsets. In truth, he wanted to share the same things with her as always, their gardening, their quiet, peaceful meals, their walks in the neighborhood, the little adventures and routines that had made it possible the last ten years for him to rise each day, to shave, to dress, to go to work.

She rode every morning, getting up before the sun broke over the horizon. She rode in the evenings after work. When winter came, she still rode on the sunny days, and on the days with snow, she rode the exercise bike at the gym. Then in the spring, she started day-long Sunday rides with a group, and then one week she broke the news that she was going on an overnighter with the group. He was stunned, floored, that she'd go away without him. She asked him to come along, but even if he could have kept up with her, the thought of sharing fellowship with strangers appalled him. The odd image that kept coming to his mind was this: he would stumble out of a tent into a foggy dawn and walk down to a creek where there

74

would be a stocky, bare-chested, bearded man brushing his teeth. The bearded man's mouth would be full of toothpaste foam and the man would point and say something garbled and roll his eyes excitedly toward the creek and the woods beyond and Henderson would look and see nothing but vague shapes in the fog, while the foamy man continued pointing in excitement.

But maybe if he'd gone on the overnighter, she would have hung back with him, coaxed him along as they labored up a hill. When they pulled into camp at the end of the day, dead last in the group, the others would have gently teased them, but kindly brought him a cup of coffee and a bowl of stew. How many years had it been since he'd had a good bowl of stew?

There was a light in her eyes these days, a spring in her step. She seemed trim and beautiful and foreign, as if he were watching her from a distance. As the spring days lengthened into summer, he found himself alone in the evenings, working in the garden. As he sank a shovel into the soil, he felt himself to be a cartoon character, mimicking, pretending to be a fellow who knew what he was doing, but he only stayed there so that she might find him upon her return, digging away, looking useful and engaged and sure of himself.

He was teaching summer classes at the university, and after his late afternoon class, he went into the library looking for some fresh lecture materials. He'd been a popular teacher for the most part, but of late he realized his lectures must be slipping because students were checking their watches almost from the get-go. It was a huge library, full of nooks and crannies, and he found himself climbing up a narrow winding staircase and coming to a set of classrooms he'd never known existed. He walked down a corridor and stared into the empty classrooms. They were carpeted, with high bookshelves and oil paintings on the walls. Cushioned seats were arranged around long oaken tables. He'd never been assigned to such elegant classrooms.

He walked down the hall and peeked though a windowed door. A professor with long wispy white hair sat at the head of the table. There were only six students at the table, sitting as if entranced, no one moving or speaking. The professor's eyes were shut, his thin hands folded over a concave chest as if he'd just been pierced and was holding in his life's blood.

The professor drifted back into the depths of his chair, and the students slipped deeper into their own seats. If they didn't rouse in a moment, they would be lost forever, trapped for all time in this hidden room in the library, cobwebs draping them and the white-haired professor.

As he descended the stairs, Henderson's heart pounded, and as he crossed the campus, his shirt clung sweatily to him. He shifted his heavy briefcase from hand to hand. His eyes took in the sandstone buildings and the red tile roofs. The sidewalks and the grassy malls were quiet on this summer evening, but he felt as if the few walkers on campus were staring at him, accusing him. Of what? What crime had he committed? On the sidewalk, a familiar looking long-haired boy on a skateboard rolled towards him. So many semesters had gone by, Henderson confused the names of past students, but this face seemed to swim at him through a haze of years as he searched his memory for the particular class he'd had the boy in, the particular seat the boy had taken. The boy was moving fast, but Henderson tried to catch his eye. Perhaps the student would say something friendly. Perhaps he would stop to chat and he would tell Henderson that he had made a difference in his life. But the student kicked his skateboard quickly past. Looking after him, Henderson had a recollection of the boy now, and he was pretty sure he had failed him. The boy had gone by a weird nickname. Antler. He'd show up stoned and fall asleep at his desk.

He was pleased somehow to know that Antler was still haunting the campus. He felt a sudden warmth and benevolence toward Antler, and he wished to join him, to skateboard down the sidewalks with him. The last time he'd ridden a skateboard was when he'd tried out the one he'd bought Joshua for Christmas. He'd recalled doing it as a kid himself, and he put one foot on as Joshua looked on encouragingly. Then Henderson kicked with his other foot, scooted forward two feet until the front of the board lifted and tossed him back in the air and he'd landed hard on his back and elbow and lay on the sidewalk with Joshua staring down at him, asking, "Are you okay, Dad? Are you okay?" Henderson smiled through the pain. "I'm fine, Joshua."

As he walked on, with Antler disappearing into the distance, Henderson crossed a footbridge with a scummy pond below. He resisted an urge to fling his briefcase into the green water, to let it sink beneath the tadpoles. He willed the papers inside to burn, to turn to ash. He would leave it all behind, his colleagues, his students, the sandstone buildings, the walkways over which he had toted the briefcase for so many years. He'd leave it all behind, start fresh with Janet.

His library search had made him arrive home later than usual, and Janet was already heading out. In her shorts and T-shirt, she looked slender and tanned and younger than her years as she rolled her bike out of the garage. She stopped as she saw him pull into the driveway.

He got out of the car, his shirt wet with sweat. She looked at him, not yet on the bike, steadying the handlebars.

He blocked her way. "I want to get a bike," he said. "I want to start riding with you."

What had he expected? A smile? An embrace? Tears came to her eyes. She was shaking her head.

She brushed past him. She mounted the bike and rode down the driveway and into the street. Henderson stood there, on a warm evening, covered with sweat, looking after her red T-shirt as she disappeared around a curve.

Later, he would ponder it. The usual metaphors. A man waking out of a dream. A man coming to his senses after a fever. It was like those things, he supposed. But those metaphors missed something. They said it all and said nothing.

He followed her in his mind as she rode through their neighborhood. He knew she crossed a street that led her to a trailhead, and then she'd ride up a dirt path through a valley that cut through the subdivision. It was settled land, but with a hint of wildness. Coyotes sometimes made appearances, and of late there had been mountain lion warnings posted on the trailheads. He'd advised her to go a different route, but she'd said she wouldn't be frightened away.

In the driveway, Henderson saw the way it would unfold. There would be months to go yet. They'd seek out counseling. But he knew one day she'd be riding with another man. He'd be a whiz. He'd know all about fixing flats, could throw up a tent in a flash, chart their rides on a global positioning system.

In the driveway, his breath leaving him in a rush told Henderson how bad it was going to be. He stood in the driveway, taking in the houses across the street, the shingle roofs, the crabapple trees, taking in the glare of the evening sunlight, noting the fading paint of his neighbor's garage door and the slant of his own driveway, the way the concrete had settled and chipped over the years.

She'd climb from the valley, cross another street and a wooden bridge and then ride around the lake. He saw her legs pumping, her face flushed with resolve, her breath hurried and then steadying as she hit her rhythm. He was proud of her. He urged her on.

The Comeback

The call came unexpectedly. I recognized the voice. Phlegmy. Breathy. Too many years of chewing tobacco. Too many years of spitting hard. Coach's question was simple: "Can you still hit the fast one?"

I hesitated. I looked at the children as they lounged on the couch watching Iron Man. A snooty space alien was trashtalking him. I was forty-four. I'd put on poundage. I spent too much time watching T.V., reading the paper, and drinking coffee. I hadn't played the game in five years.

"I don't know," I said.

"You've got a month to train," he said, and hung up.

I looked at myself sidelong in the hall mirror. I patted my thick belly. It made a sound like Thwop.

The kids promised they wouldn't do anything outlandish. I jogged through our suburban neighborhood. I sweated. I started to wheeze. When I got home, the belly was still there. It glistened with sweat. Iron Man was hanging upside down in an airless vacuum. He looked depressed.

I called Eddie, my old trainer. "I'm coming back," I said.

He hesitated. "Can you still hit the fast one?"

"I don't know," I said.

"Will you do it my way?" he said. "Will you give me all you've got and then some? Will you puke your guts out and lap it up?"

"I'm forty-four," I said.

"I'll be right over."

The kids cried. They didn't want to go to the sitter's. They liked the way we lounged about all summer while my wife went off to work. We gave each other a group hug when I dropped them off.

Eddie was waiting on my front porch. "Start running," he said. He had a beer in one hand and a pistol in the other.

"I got a little wheezy earlier," I said. "A little asthma."

He aimed the pistol. "Start running, Fat Boy. I'll trail you in the car. I'll drill you dead in the back if I don't like what I see."

I knew he might. I jogged down Griffin, then down Main. I gasped my way down Bloomsdale, where old Earl watched me from his porch. He'd fought in the war a long time ago, and it had given him the right, I suppose, to sit on his porch all day and smoke Luckys.

"What's the rush?" he called.

"Training," I panted.

"Can you still hit the fast one?"

Eddie fired off a round in his direction, and old Earl tumbled out of his deck chair, the liveliest I'd seen him in some years. Eddie came up behind me in the old Dodge. He pushed the fender against the back of my legs. He howled out the window, "Out of my way! I'll mow your ass over, Fat Boy!" He stepped on the gas and tossed me into a rose bush. He drove off honking and swearing and laughing. That was Eddie for you.

There was a message waiting on my answering machine. Eddie. He'd already found a bar. "On the floor, Fat Boy. Two hundred big ones. Break it up however you want. Then a thousand of the little crunchos. I won't ask you to do the full sitties just yet." He snapped ice around in his teeth. "Oh yeah. Better give me a cool five on the jacks." He bit a big cube in half. "Don't forget to shower. Screw this up and I'll slash your throat while you sleep."

81

I knew he would. I hit the floor, did the push-ups and crunches and jumping jacks. I was sobbing by the end, letting out little shrieks of pain and misery.

My wife came up the stairs. "What are you doing?"

"I'm coming back."

She eyed me hard. "Can you still hit the fast one?"

Eddie was at the foot of my bed when I woke up. My wife had already gone to work and had taken the kids to the sitter's. I sat up in bed and Eddie handed me something that looked like a kitchen sink. I realized it really was a kitchen sink.

"What?" I said.

"You're installing this," he said. "In my trailer."

We drove over in his old Dodge. It smelled of ancient booze and weed killer.

"Why am I installing a sink?"

"Don't play stupid," he said. "For the reflexes."

"I don't know anything about installing sinks."

"Lose the attitude. My way or the highway."

He sat in an armchair drinking beer and laughing over old Beverly Hillbillies reruns. It was the dirtiest trailer I'd ever been in. There were empty cans of tuna on stained newspapers on the floor and a dozen mangy cats rooted around licking at last morsels.

"When did you get all the cats?" I asked.

"What cats?"

My hands got all nicked and cut up. By afternoon, the sink was hooked up, but water shot out of all the joints when we turned the faucet on.

"That's okay," Eddie said. "Let me see your hands."

He flicked some cigarette ash into the cuts. "That'll seal them," he said. "Now climb up on my roof and clean off the pine needles."

82

"You got a ladder?"

"Hell no, I don't have a ladder. Start climbing."

I scratched my way up the side paneling, worked my way over an awning. A cat waited up there and bit my wrist as I crawled over the top.

I looked around. "I don't see any pine needles," I said.

"The wind must have blown them away. " He looked up at me. "Okay, stop goofing off. Jump."

I raised my eyebrows. "Jump?"

"For the calves, climberboy, if you need a reason."

I jumped. I hit the ground with a thud. Something seized in my spine and Eddie sort of rolled me to the car and got me in the back seat. He pitched me out on my front lawn. "See you at breakfast," he said. "Denny's."

So it went for a month. My wife watched my belly get trimmer. She started feeling romantic towards me again. I gave up the T.V., the paper, coffee. The kids kept their shows turned low. They looked at me in a new way. Kind of like the way they looked the first time they saw stained glass windows in church.

The big night came. Coach waited in the field. Around midnight. Only a couple of lights burned. Some of Coach's hoods stood around.

Eddie was with me. Holding my arm. My hands were shaking.

"Well?" Coach asked.

Eddie answered for me. "Give him what you got."

The fast one came out of the dark. It loomed before my eyes, large and white and luminous, beckoned to me like beautiful women and money and the roar of the crowd I'd heard once long ago, or imagined I'd heard in those blessed moments before waking. I took a step toward it as if to gather in and reclaim all that I'd once owned. Then something hammered me in the head and I was falling, my hands making a last grab into space.

When I woke, the lights were out. Eddie sat on the grass beside me, smoking a cigarette. I liked the red glow in the darkness and the sweet smell of the summer grass.

"I didn't make it," I said.

"You did good, kid," he said. "You did fine."

"Am I back?"

He chuckled low. He sighed. "You're forty-four, kid," he said. "You've been out of the game a long time."

"I thought I was coming back."

"Nobody comes back, kid. That's bullshit. That's the movies."

He flicked ash into the wound on my head, rubbed the ash in to seal it.

I lay back in the cool summer grass, sank deep into a bottomless field, and it was like the moon and the stars swallowed me up and forgave everything. I was a boy of six again, in that timeless summer of Mantle and Maris and fireflies and brothers and sisters and Momma's slow pitching, her magical southern voice drawling, "Swing, honey, swing."

The Final Conversation

This summer, at the age of forty, on vacation from the high school where I teach history, I've taken up boxing. Taken it up with a passion. Road work every day at dawn, running six miles in the cool before the heat hits. Then two or three hours in the gym, shadow boxing, punching the heavy bag, chasing the speed bag, jumping rope. Hundreds of push-ups and sit-ups.

It's the sparring, though, that really excites me, that gets the heart pounding. I'm quick on my feet. I can take a body punch. As a boxer, I have only one major flaw. I don't like hitting anybody. I'm a very polite boxer. While my opponents pound away, I flick soft jabs that graze harmlessly off their headgear. I just want to indicate that I could have hit them if I had wanted to.

After I've climbed out of the ring, sweaty from being chased around by a less polite boxer, Rudy, the gym owner and trainer, pulls me aside, drapes a heavy arm around my shoulders and says, "Dave, baby, you like to hit the heavy bag, right? I've seen you. You get a real gleam in your eye when you go after that bag. But in the ring? Dave, you are like hunted, man, it's Bambi and Godzilla, and you're playing Bambi."

"Sorry," I mutter, my voice thick through the mouthpiece. "I'm just a history teacher."

"Don't get killed out there. I got liability issues."

Around the same time I started boxing, I also started seeing a therapist. I'd never seen a therapist before. Something happened to me in the spring semester, though. I started having panic attacks. My

85

hands shook and I'd break into a sweat and get short of breath. A friend recommended Kerrie; she would work cheap, he said, because she was just out of school. "You don't need Sigmund Freud," my friend said. "Really good therapists are a pain in the ass, anyway. They get on your case."

Kerrie's a frail, long-haired young woman, and I get the feeling she's hacking away at this therapy stuff. I may be one of her first clients, but I don't mind. Maybe I'd be uncomfortable with a real pro. She works out of her house, a small upstairs apartment. I sit on a couch in her living room, and she takes an armchair. Her bedroom must be behind the bead curtain. I suspect her boyfriend's back there, lurking somewhere behind the curtain, listening. I pitch my voice out to him so he can listen in more easily. I wouldn't mind a second opinion.

We've gotten on the subject of my mother, who passed away shortly after Christmas, after a long illness.

"What was that like for you, when she died?"

"Well, I guess it wasn't unexpected."

She bites her lip, her brow furrows. I imagine it's a look therapists get when they think they're on to something. "You never really dealt with your mother's death?"

"I don't know. What does that mean? Dealt with? How do you deal with things?"

"How do you?" she asks.

I look at her. "Is that how *do* you, or how do *you*?"

She stares back at me. Lifts her eyebrows. Her chin seems to pull in a bit. "I'm not sure if I follow you."

"I'm not sure I follow me, either." I laugh. I shrug my shoulders like a boxer loosening up. I feel like making her a cup of coffee. I make great coffee.

86

Total tea drinkers recant and ask for my brew. Even my wife, who doesn't like coffee, likes my coffee. I want to tell her to sit back and put her feet up. I want to hang out here, watching the expression on her face as she drinks my coffee. I want to make my therapist happy.

Her chin juts back out a notch. She sweeps a long strand of dark hair from her face. "So how did you deal with your mother's death?"

I stare at the bead curtain, wishing someone would step out and ask for my coffee. I spread my hands. "I got sad, I guess, like anybody would. I went back to work."

Her chin juts way forward now, and her brown eyes penetrate more deeply than I'd expect from this freckle-faced young therapist. "And you went back to work," she says.

"What was I supposed to do?"

"That's the question, Dave."

"Whoa." I rise, thinking of making a break for it, crossing the livingroom, running down the stairs. I have a sense that the guy behind the bead curtain is poised to chase me down and drag me back, that that's his job. I get a tingle in the back of my neck, and I shrug my shoulders, as if to ward off the gripping hands. "Hey," I say. "I don't think I feel like talking about it anymore today."

Her eyes get a little moist, as if I've let her down, as if her big therapy moment is crashing down around her. "It's okay," I say. "Hey, can I make you a cup of coffee?"

I'm glad our house doesn't have air conditioning because I like the mugginess of summer, sweating off the pounds, getting those ropy arm muscles, at night my wife's hand running over my new hardened belly. "What's all the training for anyway?" she asks one night as we lie in bed, and I stare up in the darkness, until finally I say, "I guess I'm trying to change somehow." She holds me in the night, and I hear her breath, a little rushed, a little anxious. "What kind of change?" I feel her warmth, the press of her body against my side. The night seems to hum in around us, the sound of fans and cicadas and a car driving down the block.

I'm a stay at home Dad during the summers, though this summer I'm away a little more because of the training. I've got three boys, ages six to thirteen, and we fill in the time with bike rides and baseball and swimming and squirt gun fights and monopoly games where the youngest builds hotels on property he doesn't own, and sometimes I imagine that during the course of the day we're all going to have this great conversation. We're all going to sit out on the deck, and one-by-one we're going to talk about what we believe and what we want out of life and how much we mean to one another, and we're going to be very open and non-judgmental and full of unconditional love, and I'm going to offer all these wry insights into life...

But it's never like that, I guess. I'm crazy about my kids, but it's always chaotic, somebody's always pissed off at somebody, or gets his feelings hurt about something, and sometimes I just say *Come at me,* and we tumble into each other and roll around on the deck wrestling.

I take another pummeling at Rudy's gym, and afterwards Rudy sits beside me at ringside, while my invigorated opponent, a plump, bald middle-aged accountant, heads for the showers, tossing little punches in the air.

"I don't know, Dave, baby," Rudy says with a sigh. "I don't know if I can keep letting you back out there, man. It's supposed to be a fight, man, a *fight*. I can't just throw a victim to the wolves." Rudy's a short, very powerful Irish-Italian guy, a few years older than I am. His nose has a busted, tilted look. He trains all kinds of boxers here, a few pros but mostly amateurs, young men, old men, young women, old women. I think we've got one thing in common here. We're a little screwed up. We hit things because we don't know what else to do.

"You go in there and you slip and you duck and you weave, and you're looking pretty good, you look like you know what you're doing, you're blocking things good, you got a good block, but they're moving in on you and pretty soon you're getting the crud knocked out of you. I mean every fucking time, baby. I put you in the ring with that old lady last week, I mean what the hell is she, seventy-five? And she slaughters you, baby, she's all over your ass. I mean, when are you going to stop dancing and fight the fuck back?"

"I don't know if this has anything to do with anything," I tell my therapist. "It's just been on my mind lately."

"Go ahead," she says. She gives me one of her soft, encouraging little smiles. She's too sensitive for this kind of work. She'll get burned out. One day, somebody like me will be talking and she'll run out screaming. I don't know why she wants to do this. She should go sell real estate or something.

"There's a sun room," I say, and I talk loud enough for the guy behind the bead curtain to hear because maybe it's all a show anyway. Maybe I want a larger audience. "Or I guess you could call it a patio room. In my parents' house. It's a very white room. White tile floor. White walls. White ceiling. And all the glass windows. At night the windows reflect back at you, reflect the white room and all the people in it…"

I go on, telling her how I tried to visit more the last couple of years of my mother's sickness. My brothers and sisters come over when I'm in town, and the night I visited before she went into the hospital for the last time, we're all having supper on the enclosed patio, except for my mother, who's sick in bed. The windows are reflecting us, reflecting the table, and we're all eating, my father, me, my brothers and sisters. We're all eating like crazy, lasagna, fried chicken, meatloaf, honey-baked ham, tons of potatoes, vegetables, pies.

And then she wanders out from the bedroom, walking with an oxygen mask over her face, trailing the long air cord from the bedroom tank. She sits in her armchair in the livingroom, in her worn bathrobe, and she's so thin I think of refugee camps. She used to talk and eat and laugh with the rest of us, and now she just sits in the livingroom, staring into the sun room, watching us eat.

My fork stops in mid-air. I see us reflected in the glass, gorging ourselves, laughing.

"We should have stopped," I tell Kerrie. "We should have circled her, sat at her feet, got her to talk again. We should have remembered all the things she'd done for us. I guess I came home to have the Final Conversation, and it never happened. I never really had the Final Conversation."

"It's all right, Dave," Kerrie says. "You can cry."

But I'm not crying. I wonder what the fellow behind the bead curtain is thinking. How am I doing, fellow?

"You can cry now, Dave," she whispers, and she reaches forward and touches my hand, and my heart speeds up and my throat swells and I'm trying to tell her I'm okay, I'm just having an allergy attack or something. In a minute, I'll be better, I'll be fine, if I can just catch my breath. The bead curtain seems to wobble and pulsate and I sense the fellow behind there is going to rush out and give me CPR, but Kerrie stands over me and grips my shoulders and commands, "Breathe!" My heart slows, and my breathing evens out, and I croak through my swollen throat, "I'll make coffee."

I'm getting ready to duke it out with Blue. He's one of our best boxers, about to turn pro.

"Get him," Rudy says to me. He's in the ring, ready to ref, but he's pulling for me. He squeezes my arms, looks into my eyes. "Who are you?"

"I am Godzilla."

"Ah, shit man, you got to believe it. You sound like a history teacher."

I shut my eyes, let my voice hiss out, low and violent. "I am Godzilla."

Rudy sighs. "Better, I guess." Out the side of his mouth, I'm pretty sure I hear him whisper to some invisible angel in the ring: *Jesus, he's going to get killed.*

Blue's twenty-four and in great shape, a tall rawboned skinhead with a long jab. He has strange tattoos and piercings all over his body, and his tongue, for some reason, is blue, hence his name. When he talks, he usually says something weird and nasty. He leers at me as we touch gloves.

"Tune your piano, man," he says.

"I don't have a piano."

"Sure you do. Piano, pinata, you got 'em, man, sure do, you bet, lots of junk in the yard, no shit."

"Ignore him," Rudy says. "Drill him in the head."

Blue flicks his pierced colored tongue out at me, one of the more revolting sights I've witnessed today.

"Get him!" Rudy commands. "Attack! *Attack, attack, attack!*" With each 'attack' he chops the air with his hand.

Blue glares at Rudy. "You're showing bias," he huffs.

"Shut up," Rudy says. "I'm not showing bias. I hope he kicks your ass."

Blue tosses his left jab, effortlessly, disdainfully. I dance, I bob, I weave, but the jab catches me on the forehead, the nose, my lips. He stings me like some sadistic bee, grinning the whole time, and it's that damn grin, that leering, tongue-flicking grin, that finally releases me.

I smash those tight stomach muscles, bust up that arrogant six-pack, lash his razor ribs. I drive him back against the ropes, then I stop, spent, gasping for air.

He grins. "That's just barbecue, man. That's just barbecue."

I go berserk. Wade back in. He hangs in the ropes. I beat at his earrings. Rudy pulls me off. Blue bounces back with a grin. He leers, points a glove at my face. "I fucked your daughter in your swimming pool."

I charge at him, though it occurs to me that I don't have a daughter or a swimming pool. Rudy drags me back, pulls me through the ropes. "Easy, champ," he says. "Forget the asshole." He pulls me through the ropes, walks me toward the office, arm draped over my shoulders.

"You're the man," he says. "Ali, Marciano, Sugar Ray, Rocky, they got nothing on you, baby, you're a champ."

"I'm going pro," I say.

"Don't get carried away."

"I'm going pro," I say hotly.

"Forget about it, champ. You're a bum."

My therapist looks sad this morning. Her eyes are red and swollen.

"I'll make some coffee," I say.

"Dave," she says, "I don't want you to make coffee today."

"I thought you liked my coffee."

"Your coffee's great. But that's not why you're here. We've been avoiding this, Dave."

"What have we been avoiding?"

"The final conversation, Dave."

I sigh. I shrug my shoulders. "I'm sorry. I guess I didn't know how to tell you."

Her eyes flicker. "Just say it however. However it comes into your mind."

"Well, it's been terrific. You've helped me a lot, but I guess it's time to move on. I know I've got a ways to go, but I think I'm doing okay."

She stares at me, blinking. "You mean you're *leaving?* You're breaking off therapy?"

"I thought you..." I get it then; I realize she wasn't talking about *our* final conversation.

She closes her eyes and raises a hand to her brow, but when she opens her eyes, they have a piercing look. "Before you go," she says, "you need to have the final conversation with your mother."

I look around her sparse little apartment, my spine tingly. "I think it's a little late for that."

Her eyes narrow. "Do you have a problem with role playing?"

"I'd feel a little silly, I think."

She waves her hand toward the bead curtain. I see a shadow. I hear the sound of something dragging across the floor. If my mother were to come through

93

the bead curtain trailing her oxygen canister, I'd leap out the window. A back door quietly opens and closes.

She stares at the bead curtain. "He's gone," she says. She snatches a tissue from the coffee table and dabs at her eyes. She gives me a brave, tight little smile.

"I'm sorry," I say. I lean toward her, to embrace her trembling shoulders.

She holds a stiff arm out, her wrist bent back like a cop stopping traffic. "This isn't about me," she says.

"Of course not," I say. I move toward the kitchen. "I'll make coffee."

"Stop, Dave. Stop right there."

I turn slowly toward her and open my hands as if to catch something falling.

"Talk to her," she says, her eyes wet. "It's not too late."

The Director

     I was a part-time instructor at a small downtown college, barely making ends meet, when the Director of Humanities suddenly dropped dead of a heart attack. The Dean despised everyone in our department, but I had managed to look concerned and thoughtful at recent faculty meetings. Loathing the others, his milder contempt for me worked to my advantage and he offered me the position of Director.

     It would be a challenging job, he said, but we would go slowly. Months passed and indeed we did go slowly. Since the Dean feared sharing his power, he gave me no real duties, but I maintained a busy and harried attitude. Whenever I passed him in the corridors, I alluded to various projects I was pretending to be working on. "But there's only so much time!" I would sigh, feigning exhaustion. "It's endless!"

     He'd clap me on the shoulder and offer uplifting words such as, "We do what we can!"

     Once, though, his eyes grew glinty when he asked to see a certain nonexistent report on student recruitment which I'd been boasting about. For weeks after, I ducked into the restroom whenever I spotted him, and when we met again he'd returned to his habit of reaffirming our mutual delusion.

     We were a bottom of the barrel school in danger of losing our accreditation. Our students were mostly foreigners, or Americans who couldn't get accepted into college anywhere else, and our teachers spent their office hours preparing resumes for other jobs. I was forced to evaluate a teacher one day, and I sat in the back of his class as his droning voice produced a profound numbness in my head. Looking around, I saw that our students had turned numb, too. The monologue of the teacher drifted forth, traveling through the musty corridors, escaping out the windows onto the streets of our city, catching innocent bystanders unaware and numbing them as well.

The downtown of our city contained a wonderful mix of humanity. There were students from our school and from the major university a few blocks away. There were business types, street musicians, jugglers, skateboard riders, teenagers with Mohawk haircuts, people whizzing by in motorized wheelchairs. From Chinese and Arab street vendors, people would buy coffee, donuts, egg rolls, falafels, and sit on the iron benches in the Square, enjoying the sunny brisk winter air, feeding crumbs to the pigeons and listening to the haunting strains of a violin rising over the honking of taxis.

I was better paid after my promotion, and as I walked down the sidewalks on my breaks from school, I gave out change to the panhandlers who leaned against storefront windows in and around Constitution Square. I relished my role; here my good man, here is a quarter. It was very snooty, really, this sort of munificence, but I gave money—usually a quarter—to anyone who asked. After all, I was the Director of Humanities.

But there was one homeless man who never asked for money. I saw him nearly every day, and he stood out because even for the homeless he seemed badly off. He didn't wear any shoes, and his feet were caked with dried blood. One filthy pant leg was raggedly cut off below his knee, and the other pant leg ended just above his scabby ankle. He wore a rag of a t-shirt and always carried a green woolen blanket over his shoulders, a thin defense against the winter cold. Though our climate was mild, I'd heard of homeless people dying of exposure in our city, but I thought there must be organizations he could ask for help. Places

96

where he could go and get a meal, a pair of shoes, a coat, shelters where he could spend the colder nights.

He was so tall and thin that his legs reminded me of pelican legs. His greasy hair was long and scraggly and he wore a headband to hold it back. The headband was the only clothing he ever changed; on some days he wore a red headband and on other days a green one. I had the queasy feeling that upon waking each day he would spend time deciding on the green or red headband for the day.

On some days, he walked rapidly through the square, his eyes focused on the distance as if he were on a mission. On other days, his emaciated legs bore him fitfully down the sidewalk. He would walk a few steps, stop abruptly, and put his hands to his face as if he had just recalled something alarming.

One day in the square, some teenagers snuck up on the man and tugged on a corner of his green blanket. He turned and threw a wild, fierce haymaker over the boys' heads and as the boys laughed and backed away, he continued down the street, yelling now, a hoarse wordless sound of outrage, betrayal, and defiance.

But for a while, I didn't think all that much about the green blanket man, as I called him in my mind. He was just another lost soul I passed by as I took my downtown strolls. Daily, I left the school and bought a cup of coffee in the square. The coffee was a wonderful, strong French Roast and a cup or two elevated me from my chronic hungover fog. Suddenly I would be aware of sounds, colors, delicious aromas, the beat and hum and throb of humanity pressing into Constitution Square—and then the bittersweet strains of the violin. I wore a tweed coat now, and it felt good to be out and about. My little stroll, you know, wearing my tweed coat, handing out my quarters like the magnanimous fellow that I was.

When I gave money, I sometimes felt my eyes tear up, but I'm not sure if it was out of sympathy for the panhandlers or in appreciation of my own relentless humanity. But as the weeks passed, I stopped giving money to everyone. If a person seemed crazy, sometimes I wouldn't give anything, thinking, "Money won't help *you.*"

But the green blanket man never asked anyone for money. I wondered about him. There were secrets he must know, secrets of survival and living on the edge. What must he think of people like me?

Towards February, I noticed him sitting often in the square, near the entrance to the subway. He sat on a brick wall that enclosed a couple of saplings. Now that he was sitting, rather than in motion, he seemed to have declined, grown more tired. He coughed constantly, covering his mouth and making almost no sound as his chest and shoulders spasmed.

I often walked past the brick wall that he sat on. At first, I can't say that he ever looked directly at me. He never reacted in any physical way to my presence, and yet I thought that he had noticed me. My neck and shoulders always tightened as I stopped a few feet away to buy my coffee from the vendor. I sometimes thought of buying him a cup and handing it to him. But I didn't.

Where did he sleep? I wondered. I was always seeing stories in the news about homeless people sleeping in doorways or in parks, but what the hell was that really like? How could anybody stand that?

On a cold, drizzly night, after I'd had a lot to drink, my custom at the time, I told my wife that I was going out in the back yard to spend the night. Why? she wanted to know. So that I would have some idea of what it was like, I told her, so that I would know. First she laughed, thinking I was joking. When I carried a blanket out and lay down on the soggy grass, she yelled at me to come in. Then she came out carrying her own blanket and lay down beside me. I was already wet and trembling and miserable and I realized that I would soon need another whiskey. I said that I could not permit her to freeze and that we must go in.

She said that she wasn't going in. My wife suffered from a certain rare form of hysteria, which the untrained eye could not detect. When her fits came over her, she did not cry or scream, but she was hysterical all the same and beyond reasoning. Why can't you go in? I asked. Because I want to know, she moaned, I want to know, I want to know, I want to know.

I half-pulled, half-wrestled her to her feet and managed to get her back inside the house.

The green blanket man began to meet my eye whenever I walked past his brick wall. He lifted his eyes and stared at me, giving me a look that said: *You're a pig.* Throngs of other people walked past, but he reserved this particular look for me. Out the corner of my eye, I would note his shoulders straighten a notch when he caught sight of me. His neck stretched upwards and his body tilted forward and he gave me his look: *You're a pig.*

I quit walking through Constitution Square. I looped over to University Avenue instead. There were no outdoor vendors there and I had to buy my coffee inside a cafe; the coffee was weak and tasteless and failed to work its magic. Too, I missed the violin music in the square. After a couple of weeks, I tried my old walk again and he wasn't on the brick wall.

For a couple of weeks, I hardly thought of him. My wife and I had some long talks and I agreed to drink less. We talked of the garden we would plant in the spring; we talked of having a child one day. My wife, a secretary, also volunteered at the hospital. She brought me along with her sometimes and we sat in the rooms of the ill and listened to their laments. My wife was very good with the ill, patting their hands and saying soothing things. Once, a man collapsed in the corridor and the doctors and nurses gathered around him and pounded on his chest.

Sometimes my office mate Albert joined me on my daily strolls. Albert wore a tweed coat, too, and we walked down the street together dispensing change like a couple of English lords. One day we'd bought coffee and donuts and Albert cast his eyes about the square, at the panhandlers and the teenagers with their ill-advised haircuts and said, with a chuckle, "Why must we associate with the rabble?"

Just then the green blanket man hurried by on the sidewalk, weaving his way through the crowd, eyes focused on the distance, walking rapidly as he carried out some important mission. He swept past us without noticing me and I looked after his retreating back, noting the dried blood and scabs on the backs of his legs.

"He's alive," I said, pointing him out to Albert. "He's been hanging around here for weeks. He doesn't even wear shoes."

"Yeah, it's terribly sad," Albert said. "But I guess there's nothing we can do about it."

He shook his head and made a sad face, and I shook my head and sighed, and we looked at each other and giggled and took bites out of our donuts.

"I guess the whole world's gone to hell," Albert said, and we chuckled all the way back to school.

The next day the green blanket man was back on the red brick wall, but he didn't look up at me as I stopped to buy my coffee. His blanket was draped over his shoulders, and his head hung down and swayed from side to side as he hummed tonelessly. His long, dirty hair hid his face and he looked drooped over and listless.

I sipped my coffee and stared directly at him, and he glanced up suddenly and met my eye as if he'd known all along that I was there. But he didn't give me his old insulting look. He'd been beaten up. A purplish knot rose grotesquely from his forehead and one eye was swollen shut. He leaned forward as if he might topple into my arms. I shuddered, threw my coffee in a wastebasket, and hurried back to school.

In our office, I told Albert about the pleading look the man had given me. "My God, Albert, I think he's *dying,*" I said. "I've been watching a man die all semester without doing anything about it."

Albert looked up from the papers he was grading and said, "Lighten up. It's not *your* problem, is it?"

In a discussion in my literature class that day, a foreign student asked me to explain my "philosophy of life." I wobbled before the class. I felt like rushing him. I heard myself say that we should live our lives with courage and kindness. My foreign students looked at me as if I had spoken great words; a few applauded. I had to hurry out of the classroom and into the bathroom, where I sat in a closed cubicle, my body trembling.

I started drinking a lot at night again, and the evenings were very hazy. I'd get drunk and shout at the television and my wife would wander from room to room. She'd try to get me to eat, but I'd hardly touch supper, and I'd wake in the night in bed with my heart beating fast, not remembering the end of the evening. I would listen to my wife breathing, making sure she was all right. Once she wasn't in bed and I rose and found her in the bathroom, curled in the fetal position on the cold tile floor. I lay down beside her and held her as she shivered. I whispered over and over again that I was sorry, but she lay without responding, as if she hardly knew me.

On the streets, I stopped giving out money. On the sidewalk one day, a tall woman with a scarf wrapped around her head grabbed my arm and shrieked, *"Should a child stay with his mother or father?"*

"I don't give a shit!" I shouted back.

In the office I told Albert about this new feeling that had come over me, this feeling of hostility towards the panhandlers and the homeless and the crazy people walking the streets. "I hate them!" I said. "Why don't they all move?"

"Yeah, I know where you're coming from," Albert said.

I should have quit walking through the Square, but I needed to know, from day to day, if the green blanket man was still alive. As spring neared, I looked at him with a certain hope. Perhaps if he made it through winter, he would be okay. Maybe the whole winter would simply seem like a bad dream. In the spring, I'd get sober. I'd prepare my classes better and perhaps I'd really work on all those projects I'd been pretending to work on. I'd win back the favor of the Dean, who hardly even nodded to me in the corridors any more.

In my boozy fog, sometimes I envisioned a delightful future for the green blanket man and me. With my help, he would secure a small loan and he would open a flower store. Bougainvillaea blooming in the windows of his store—light shining through a sun roof—a pot of coffee in a rear room. The green blanket man still dressed in rags—but more as symbol now—clean rags and no blood on his legs. My God, in fact the green blanket man has a wonderful tan—he's just back from Brazil—business, you know. Rare seeds. We greet customers together and he touches me tenderly on the back of my neck.

The green blanket man no longer gave me an insulting look when I walked past him, nor did he look to me for help. Rather, he looked at me now in a kind of indifferent resignation. That look bothered me most of all, and one day I tossed the last of my coffee in a trash basket and suddenly approached him and held out a dollar. He looked at my hand, at the dollar held between my thumb and index finger. His lips pursed and he made a noise in his throat, and then he spat on my hand. He turned his head away without taking the money. My whole body shook and I had to stuff my hands back in my pockets of my tweed coat to keep from hitting him.

The next day I brought him another dollar. I had been sleepless all night thinking about the incident, and I was ready this time. If he spat on my hand again, I would hit him. I would grab him by the throat and drag him off his wall and hit him over and over and over.

I held the dollar out and he looked at me with a calm expression, working his tongue against the side of his mouth as if he had food caught in his teeth. Slowly he reached out and took the dollar, looked it over as if checking to see if it was counterfeit, and then stuffed it into his dirty pants. He gave me a long look, nodding his head with a condescending smile on his lips. I was crazy, the look said, I was all screwed up.

I started going to a new cafe in the other direction. One day I sensed that I was being followed and I looked back and saw him half a block behind me, as always carrying his ratty green blanket. I walked fast, turned a corner, and hurried back to school.

A few days later I was returning from another stroll. I turned off the busy avenues and walked down the quiet side street where our school was located. As I walked up the steps to the front entrance, I heard a high, whinnying laugh, and I whirled and saw him watching me from across the street.

"Get out of here!" I shouted.

Just as I shouted, the Dean stepped out the front door of the school and drew to a startled stop on the steps. He gave me a look of stark disapproval, as if I were bringing ruin down upon our sacred school. Then shaking his head, he brushed by me and started down the street. I followed him, saying, "Let me explain," but he only waved his hand over his shoulder, without looking back, calling out, "Not to worry. Perfectly understandable." He tugged his overcoat tightly about him and hurried on through the gray, drizzly afternoon, and when I turned sluggishly back toward the school, the green blanket man had already disappeared.

Back in my office, I told Albert about making a fool of myself in front of the Dean. "Gee, that's too bad," Albert said. He snickered through his nose. "Maybe we could get the green blanket man a basketball scholarship."

When I got home that night, I got drunk very quickly. I rampaged around the house like a rhino as I raged to my wife about the green blanket man. What should I do? I demanded of her. Give him money? Ignore him? Kill him? Bring him into our home?

She was making a noodle dish, and she kept stirring the noodles in a certain detached way as they slowly burned up. "We're not going to make it, are we?" she said. And then she said it, again and again, as the noodles burned.

In the night, the temperature dropped and a light snow fell. In the morning, I drove to work earlier than usual, just after dawn.

I wanted to sit alone in my office and let my mind clear. I parked and walked down the slippery, icy sidewalk towards the front entrance.

Across the street from our school, he was sleeping on the sidewalk, green blanket draped over him. I watched his motionless figure for a few moments, then took a breath, crossed the street and shook his shoulder. He smelled rotten and of liquor. Damn drunk, I thought, though I was hungover myself.

He didn't move. I stepped back and quickly crossed the street and went inside my office. The building was empty except for the custodian, a dour silent man who was rumored to have been, some twenty years before, the old Director of Humanities. He had fallen out of favor with the Dean those many years ago, had been fired, and had come back begging for a job. The Dean had taken away his textbooks and put a broom and a dustpan in his hands.

I sat in my office for half an hour, reading and re-reading a personal essay entitled, "The Time I Got Chickenpox." Finally I marked an "A" on the paper, scribbled *Fascinating* across the top and pushed it into a pile with others of its despicable ilk. By this time, I could hear other people moving around in the hallways. Albert stuck his head in and said hello and then wandered off to the canteen.

I went back outside to make sure the green blanket man had gotten up, but he was still lying there. The street was livelier now, but it was still quiet. I watched the man from the front steps as a few cars passed without slowing. A man walking by paused over the green blanket man. He bent over him, then thought better of it, shook his head and went on his way.

Finally I crossed the street. I shook his shoulder gently, and then more vigorously.

From the steps of our school, the Dean called, "What's going on here?"

"He's passed out," I said.

105

"Come inside," he said. "We don't want any trouble."

"I think we'd better call an ambulance."

The Dean compressed his lips and disappeared inside.

I rolled him over, swept his long hair back from his face, and saw that his headband was missing; it seemed a profoundly shabby thing that someone had stolen his headband. His face had a bluish tint, but I thought I heard a low strangled sound in his throat. I put my ear to his mouth, listening for a breath. Kneeling over him, I struck him hard on the chest and then again. The Dean shouted from across the street, "Get away from him, you fool!" I thought I heard another low wheeze, and I lowered my mouth to the man's lips as I lifted his chin and tilted his head back. But the moment my lips brushed his dry cracked lips, a foul odor rose up at me; a black wave came over me and my head spun dizzily. I moved my head to the side, gagging with nothing coming up.

The ambulance arrived without even using its siren. It was the most routine of calls, and the two attendants moved slowly, making a couple of comments about the green blanket man's stench as they put him on the stretcher and covered his head with the sheet. A policeman had appeared by then, and he took my statement with the greatest boredom.

"Did you know him?" he asked.

"No," I said. "I never saw him before in my life."

When I walked across the street, some of our students were clustered there watching me. They parted to let me through and I stood over my desk, gripping the edge of the desk so that my hands wouldn't shake so badly.

Albert came in and put his hand on my shoulder. "It's very tough," he said. "But I think the fact that you cared that much is a very healthy sign."

I crossed the room and swept his neatly stacked books off his desk.

"It's okay," he said. "I understand. I can relate."

I whirled and hit him in the stomach. He doubled over and clutched his belly just as the Dean stepped into our office. As I came toward the Dean with my fists clenched, his eyes grew wide. "Not to worry," he said. "Perfectly understandable," and I knew that, as of that moment, I was no longer the Director.

Dinsmore's Paradox

My younger brother Sean and I both had our own apartments in San Antonio, but on most Sunday afternoons that summer, we met at our parents' house, the house we'd grown up in. At one of our family gatherings, my mother remarked that Sean looked thin. He'd always been slender, but I had to agree with her that he looked frail.

"Are you vegetarian again?" my mother asked.

He smiled. "No, Mom. Don't worry about me. I'm fine."

My father was busy somewhere, but Sean and my mother and I sat at the round dining table in the glassed-in patio that jutted into the backyard. Despite my mother's gentle but rather persistent proddings, he would not eat, though he did drink several glasses of iced tea. My mother studied Sean's handsome, boyish face. His blue eyes held a sharp glitter. Her eyebrows drew closer together. "Are you on something, Sean? Drugs?" She glanced toward the interior of the house, listening for my father's approach. She whispered, "You can tell me."

He laughed. "I'm not on anything, Mom. You know me better than that."

She sighed, dropped a napkin to the table in her fading southern lady role. 'I don't know," she said, rolling her eyes to the heavens. "I don't know if I do."

He smiled and placed his hand over hers. It was the sort of gesture that would have made him a great priest, the calling he'd abandoned before making his final vows. "Of course you do. I'm not on anything."

She gave me a hard look, a look that clearly said, you are most definitely your younger brother's keeper. "Is he on anything?"

"Come on, Mom. You know Sean's not on anything. All his money goes to buy my dope."

She reeled back, in mock horror, as Sean and I giggled. We had a way of reverting around my mother, of turning back into supercilious teenagers.

"Well, aren't you both just a couple of spitfires." She frowned. "I'm making an appointment for you with Dr. Glover. There's something wrong here."

"What's wrong?" my father asked. He stood in the opening between the patio and the living room. He had a way of appearing just in time to hear interesting snatches of conversation.

"Sean's too thin. He's lost weight," my mother said.

"Well, give him something to eat." My father pulled on his work gloves and headed out to the garden.

"Will you see Dr. Glover? If I make the appointment for you?"

Sean covered her hand again. "I'll be fine, Mom."

The afternoon wore on. Sean drank glasses of water and sweetened tea. My mother got out her photo albums. There were my parents the year before in England. There were my parents in Paris. They grinned cheerily in all the photos. Their London Fog coats gave them a dapper, citizens of the world air, but Sean and I knew about the missed trains, the panicky wanderings through rough London neighborhoods. We knew about my mother's asthma attacks, the wrecked rental car, the pickpocketing in Rome. There had been blunders, mishaps. It had been a good and exciting time to be sure, but the carefree worldly couple in the pictures had never existed.

Later in the afternoon, Sean and I walked up the hill in our neighborhood of ranch and two-story brick homes. The temperature was in the high nineties, but there was a cloud cover and the air was soft and moist. We had grown up in this neighborhood, but I hadn't spent much time here since going away to college a decade before. I was in San Antonio once again, trying to decide if I was staying or leaving, but the old neighborhood didn't feel like mine anymore. There weren't any kids out, just people my parents' age, out watering their lawns.

"So what's going on?" I asked. "Are you okay?"

"I've been fasting."

"Why?"

We climbed higher up the hill. His breath was short. He chuckled. "For the sins of the world."

We often adopted a melodramatic means of conversing with one another, but I wasn't sure what to make of this. He'd been in the seminary for several years before finally deciding not to become a priest.

He put an arm around my shoulder. "I don't know how to tell Mother this, Tim, so I guess I'll try it out on you. I'm going to Africa."

I looked at him, moving out from under his arm so that I could stare at him. "Africa? Are you serious?"

"I've been accepted by the Maryknolls. As a lay teacher. I guess my fasting has been my way of getting spiritually ready." He laughed. "But I don't know if I'm scared of going away or scared of telling Mom."

"Jesus, Sean. This is going to shake her up, all right."

"This is selfish, isn't it?" he said gloomily. "It's going to make her unhappy."

"Of course it is. You're screwing it up for everybody. Now I'll be bored without you around, so I'll have to move again. Then they'll be disappointed in me."

110

"Do you blame me for going?"

"Of course I blame you. You get all the glory in this damn family. Why couldn't you be a drunk or something so I could get a little credit? All this Saint Francis of Assissi crap makes me sick."

He laughed as we headed down the hill for home. "I'm hungry," he said.

Ten years later, I really did feel like blaming him for something. Mother's emphysema, which had been diagnosed some years before, had taken a turn for the worse. Sean was somewhere in Chiapis,, Mexico, and we couldn't reach him. My mother, from her hospital bed, in between her gasping breaths, kept asking about him. She stayed lucid until the end and had read in the newspaper a few days before, a story about a massacre by paramilitary thugs in a Chiapis village. "How do we know he's not rotting in some shallow grave?" she kept inquiring, repeating this theme so often that, despite her illness, I wanted to scream at her to desist.

As on other of his missions in the last years since leaving the Maryknolls, he was only loosely allied with any humanitarian organization, though he was usually fairly good about staying in touch. There would be calls from foreign lands or e-mails might arrive from the most unlikely places. He usually told us after the fact of his arrival in tough places, not before, so that there would be no time for us to protest his putting himself in danger.

This time, though, he had called me at my home in Portland, from the train station in Mexico City, just before he left for Chiapis.

"Are you out of your mind?" I asked. "That's a hotbed down there right now."

He chuckled. "I've been worse places, Tim. I'll be fine. I wish you could come with me."

"Oh sure. I'll tell Jane. I'm sure she'll be delighted to have me go off to Mexico. I'll tell her right now. She's getting the kids out of the bath. They'll all be happy to hear it."

He laughed. "I know you can't come. Your place is with your family."

I sighed. "I guess I envy your adventures."

"I guess I envy you, too. Beautiful wife and kids. Nice home in suburbia. Golden lab."

"It's a cocker spaniel if you didn't notice." I paused. "I wish you'd become a priest. At least we'd know where you were most of the time."

There was an unusual silence for us then, and for once neither of us leapt into the gap. Finally he said, "I guess I would have become one if I had the right kind of faith."

I had a bad feeling about Chiapis, so I played my trump card. "Mom's going to be worried."

He chuckled. "I was waiting for your trump card."

"It's your play."

"I have no response."

"Oh, you bastard," I said. "Very clever. Now I'm to feel guilty for trying to make you feel guilty."

"Exactly. Dinsmore's Paradox."

"Dinsmore's Paradox. Brilliant." Of course we both knew there was no such thing.

"My train's here," he said.

"What a load. 'My train's here.' I know that's the sort of dramatic closing line you like. 'My train's here.' "

He laughed. "Tim, my train really is here."

"Call me as soon as you can. Collect."

"I will."

Into the moment of stillness before we hung up, I said, "I have some last words for you. Come home."

I got off before he could respond, but I immediately I felt guilty for guilt tripping him.

He'd been in Chiapis for three weeks, out of touch, when my father called me to tell me my mother had been hospitalized. She'd been in the hospital several times before, but most of the time I only heard after the fact. "Mom was in the hospital last week," my father would call to say. "But don't worry. She's okay now." In the background, I'd hear my mother asserting, "Give me the phone. Give me the phone..." Then she'd get on. "Now you are not to worry," she'd say in her best the south-will-rise-again voice. "You take care of Jane and those little angels of yours. We'll be fine here. Just fine."

But this time there was a quaver in my father's voice that alarmed me, even though as usual they told me not to worry. I wasn't buying it this time. I was coming home.

It was a bad time to leave. Jane had just come down with the flu and there were our two little kids to take care of. She was running a hundred and three fever.

"Should I go home?"

"Of course you should," Jane said. She coughed thickly and moaned from the couch where she lay. "I'm okay."

"What should I do?"

"Go. This will only last for a few days. If you're not there, you'll blame yourself forever."

I sat on the couch, stroking her feverish head. Her back spasmed with chills. "Just get a nurse in here," she gritted through her shaking teeth. "Get a full medical team."

I arranged for sitters and friends to help out. The next morning the children got into the thick of things. They clutched at my trousers as the airport shuttle honked from the driveway.

"Bring me a shiny pistol, Daddy!" Tommy cried. He was four, but somehow he sensed that Texas might be the very place to pick up the shiny toy pistol he'd set his sights on.

"We'll see, Tommy."

'Promise!"

"Okay, okay."

"Shiny pistol!" Sam, two, echoed.

What opportunists! We had tried to keep toy guns out of the house, but now I would promise an arsenal. I kissed Jane and the boys and ran out the door, waving at the waiting shuttle driver.

By the time I arrived, she was lapsing in and out of consciousness, and her doctors had indicated the time was short, a few days at most. She knew it, and her main concern was with Sean. I'd stopped briefly back at the family house for a shower and a change of clothes when he finally called. The Red Cross had gotten a message to him.

"How's Mom?" he asked.

I took a breath, as if to say it was to finally admit it. "I'm sorry, Sean. She's dying. It won't be long."

There was a silence on the other end. Then he said, "It's going to take me a little while, Tim. I'll get there as soon as I can." His voice trembled. "The situation here is a little dangerous."

Suddenly we were five and nine again, and I was the big brother on the top bunk keeping the ghosts and monsters away. I was the big brother straightening the handlebars on the fallen bike and leading a sniffling, bloody-kneed little brother home.

"Do you want me to come get you?"

He laughed. "You would." His voice grew stronger. "I'll get there."

He was good to his word. He arrived at the hospital, panting as if he'd been running, hair mussed, doing his best brother-home-from-the-wars routine, just hours before her death. My mother, eyes flickering open and shut, oxygen mask on her face, squeezed his hand. It was not quite the perfect closing; in the more perfect closing, she might have removed the oxygen mask and whispered, once more, the last words she'd actually spoken to me the day before. My father had been out in the hallway, belaboring a nurse, off on some mission of his own creation, when she opened her eyes, drew me close, and rasped in her best, her very best southern lady dying voice, the very last words she ever spoke to me. She shut her eyes after she said it, as if she'd gotten it right, didn't want to tamper with the closing. I kissed her forehead, knowing even then it was a gift, something to carry with me into the future. I love you, she'd said. I love all of you.

On the day after the funeral, my father and Sean and I went back to the cemetery. It was a beautiful warm morning in April, the sky clear. Sprinklers twirled on the broad expanse of grass. I kept looking at the date's on my mother's gravestone. Sixty-six years old. The arc of a life. Born in the Depression. Born before television, the advent of the computer. Born on a ranch once burned down by the Comanches in her grandmother's time. A war bride. A mother. A secretary. A college student at the age of sixty.

The land was open and flat here, running away to the horizon, spotted by a few lone oaks. Sean told me that he'd dreamed he'd spent the night here at the cemetery, sitting beside our mother's grave. Ghosts had visited him in the dream, dead grandparents and aunts and uncles, a cousin lost in our youths.

115

Perhaps it's strange to say, but the week after my mother's death was a happy one. There had been tears, to be sure, but my mourning would be a long and quiet one, my sense of loss creeping over me in unguarded moments, a wave of sadness rather than a tempest. My father was glad to have us both home again, and he was busy responding to calls and cards and flowers, and our company and the busyness of the post-funeral time had kept him from staring too hard into the future. Sean and I took long walks through the neighborhood, exploring old haunts, recalling the friends who had lived in the various houses, though by now even most of our friends' parents had moved away. In the warm afternoons, we played basketball at our old playground.

Our bunks were no longer in our old room, and each night we carried blankets and pillows out to the patio and slept there. One night he shook me awake.

Still lying on the floor, we watched through the glass as two animals chased each other up, down, and around a tree. I thought it was squirrels at first, huge squirrels, but as my eyes focused, two recognizable shapes formed. "Raccoons!" Sean whispered.

"Raccoons!" I whispered back. We had not seen raccoons in our neighborhood since we were kids. They chased and cavorted about, then they drank from the rock pond and slipped back into the darkness.

We stared up at the stars, visible through the skylight. "It's been great to be with you again," he said. "I've been lonely."

"You could come stay with us in Portland. Jane and the kids would love it."

He sighed. "I wish I could. But I've got to go back."

I thought to argue, but all I said was, "The priest returns to his parishioners."

116

He shifted his head on his pillow. "No. Just a regular guy. I don't even know anymore who or what I'm praying to sometimes."

"That makes two of us, I guess."

An acorn dropped on the skylight and rattled down the roof. He folded his hands over his chest and looked up at the stars. "I'm glad we saw the raccoons again."

A couple of days later, we'd finished eating lunch on the patio. Light flooded into the room and made the white floor tiles gleam. Every couple of minutes an acorn fell and clattered down the roof. My father and I idled over our iced tea, an uncharacteristically calm moment for my father, while Sean was down the hallway on the phone, making arrangements for his return to Chiapis.

We heard the murmur of his conversation in the background. My father frowned and looked at me. "Why didn't he become a priest?" he asked, as if I were privy to the secret.

I glanced away, looking across the lawn, wishing I might spy a raccoon peeking out of the shrubbery. Then I shrugged my shoulders. "He said once he didn't have the right kind of faith."

My father, a man of perpetual internal and external motion, looked suddenly very still in the sunlight, his hand holding a glass of iced tea in mid-air. "What on earth did he mean by that?"

But there was Sean now, in the opening between the patio and the living room. He stood before us, handsome, tall, slender. From our chairs, we looked up at him as he stood there, a kind of tired light in his eyes on that day some months before he disappeared in the rain forests of Chiapis, on a supply run between town and village. "I'm ready," he said.

Transformations

The movies and the books get it all wrong, with their stories of bad people who turn saintly. In reality, the shallow cold-hearted fellow does not transform, does not warm up or grow tender. No, the years go by and he is more lost and unbearable than ever.

But wait, wait. Soon the film becomes unwatchable, the book unreadable. After all, we must have a transformation, a change of heart.

Let's take Paul, a hard thug of a guy who's drinking in a bar with some of the boys. He's getting ripped. It's a rough bar, full of drug dealers, bikers, ex-cons and embittered war veterans. Lots of scars in this crowd, kidney disease, enlarged livers, heart arrhythmias. Seedy, smoky types. People puke in the bathrooms. Fights break out at the tables, sex acts take place in the dark corners. It's the sort of place Paul knows too well. At thirty-three he's banged around from town to town, worked shit jobs, spent time in county jails for drunkenness and fighting and petty thievery. He's been on the road, but finds himself passing through his old hometown. His parents are dead, he hasn't stayed in touch with any friends of his youth. He's lonely as hell, though that's not a feeling he'd admit to in this crowd. He worked with some of these guys today, day labor at a warehouse. They're okay guys, some of them, but he'll get back on the road tomorrow. Nothing left for him here.

The television is on above the bar for those not presently puking, fighting, or engaging in sex acts in the dark corners. There, on the screen, in a show with no discernible plot, Paul sees her. His old flame. No, of course it's not really her. But it looks like her. His girlfriend from his teen years. Grown up now, like him,

118

but nicely grown. Still pretty, but what he sees in her face is kindness. And though he can't hear what she's saying, she appears to be saying something nice to a young man who is distressed. She strokes his hair in a gentle sort of way. Paul stares at the distressed young man and at the pretty woman kindly stroking his hair, and he feels a sharp stab in his chest, a stab of memory and loss and longing, the kind of pain he's guarded himself from for years with booze, dope, cheap thrills in cheap motels.

"I knew a nice girl once," he says.

The guys press in close to him at the bar, respond with great empathy and profound understanding. One man belches and rubs at his crotch. "Oh yeah, I bet she was nice," he says. "Real nice. I knew her too."

"Oh yeah," a tattooed man says, "She was real nice. Real nice."

"I knew her too," a man on his left says. "Real nice. Sweet lips."

"We all knew her," a metal-studded biker from down the bar calls. "Real nice."

Sudden tears spring into Paul's eyes. "Fuck you."

Their obscene hoots rush him out the door like a boot in the ass, and he stumbles into the cold January night, into this first snowfall of the new year, the tears running down his cheeks.

What had happened to him? How had he blown it so badly? She'd been a nice girl and she'd loved him, and he'd let her slip away. Hell, he'd forced her away, with his dealing and his drugging and his running wild. He'd done a couple of years in the army to get out of a jam, and when he came back to town she was long gone, married, off to a new state, and for years he'd had dreams that they'd both come back to town at the same time. In his visions, her marriage hadn't worked out

119

and he'd get clean and sober and they'd get back together and he'd settle down, get a regular job. But he hadn't dreamed of her in a long time. He hadn't even thought of her in a long time before he saw the woman on the television stroking the hair of the distressed young man.

He walks down the street to his car, feeling her hand stroking his own face. It's too late, he knows that she's not coming back, but he suddenly knows where it all went wrong, where it all started, where he began to live the kind of life that drove her away. He bends over, scoops snow up and wipes it into his face. He's not going to drink anymore tonight. Maybe he won't drink tomorrow. He needs to think about this. He needs to be clear-headed. He needs to do something now, tonight. He can drive. He's sober enough to drive. Well, maybe not legally, but the streets around here are nearly vacant of traffic, the good folks already home in bed or in front of their televisions. He hopes Mr. Mitchell is up. Mr. Mitchell has got to be up.

He has to work with his car door to get in. It's wired up, doesn't close properly, and one of the taillights is out; he hopes a cop doesn't spot that. But he's got to risk it. It's not a large town. He can be back in the old neighborhood in a few minutes. He drives with the windows down, the cold air sobering him up.

He'd been seventeen on the night of his first real crime. He was out riding with two friends when they'd decided to burglarize Mr. Mitchell's house. He'd never broken into a house before. He'd never even shoplifted, though he'd hung out when his friends did. They had a bottle in the car and some pot. That was pretty new to him, too, though not entirely so. Suzy didn't like it when he drank or smoked, so he kept it to a minimum, though his friends ragged him that he was pussy-whipped. He'd guessed so, though he loved her so that made it worthwhile.

120

He hadn't really wanted to rob the house, but he hadn't put up much of an argument against it. They were just driving around, drinking on a Friday night, when the idea had come up. They knew that Mr. Mitchell and his son, Ned, who played on the high school basketball team, would be at Ned's game that night. Mr. Mitchell always sat in the front row of the gym and hopped up and applauded like crazy when Ned sank a shot. He wasn't a jerk about it though. He didn't berate Ned or anybody else when they flubbed up. Mrs. Mitchell had died some years ago. Ned was a decent guy. They'd smoked dope with him a couple of times, but they weren't really friends of his, not enough to worry about causing any great harm to him by robbing his house. They wouldn't make a mess. They'd just take a few things. The family might not even notice for a while. Ned seemed to have some money. He drove a nice car and dressed nice. Danny, the only one who really wanted to rob the house and who seemed to have just a little something against Ned, said that on the east side of the house there was a window that was obscured from the road by an oak tree and some hedges. He was right. They crawled in under the hedges and there the window was and they couldn't be seen from the street. "I don't want to break a window," Paul said. He did say that, he was sure. Even years later, he recalled saying that and he gave himself some credit for that. But as luck would have it, the window was not locked.

He doesn't have any trouble finding Mr. Mitchell's house. It's only a few blocks from the house he grew up in, the house his parents had left him and his brother. They'd sold the house and split the money, and his share was long gone. His brother was out in California, in computers. His brother was okay, a decent guy, but he made Paul feel bad with his nice house, nice wife, nice kids. Hell, even their dog was nice. He'd visited a couple of years before, but he could tell he made Jim's wife uneasy and when he'd left there he'd felt sadder and more alone than he had in years. Maybe he'd try again. Jim had promised to help him get a job whenever he wanted. Jim even wanted to send him back to college. Maybe he would go to college, goddamn it, he bet there'd be some good-looking women to bang.

He doesn't park right in front of the brick ranch-style house. He parks across the street and a few houses down. There's still time to change his mind. This is crazy. This is a bad idea. His heart pounds. Sweat springs out on the back of his hands and underneath the rim of his ski hat.

There's a porch light on, and a light in the livingroom. Fuck it. Do it, just do it. He knows if he doesn't do it now, he's never going to do it. It's tonight or never, and somehow as he steps out of the creaky car door into the cold night, he knows he's always been working his way back here. Every drunk, every night in a jail cell, every stupid senseless brawl, has been calling him back to this moment. He looks across the street at the house. It's exactly the same. There's the oak tree and the hedges along the eastern wall. For a mad moment, it occurs to him to change the game plan, to crawl through the hedges and go in through the window and rob Mr. Mitchell again. Hell, his funds are low. He'll tie Mr. Mitchell up. He won't hurt him, just tie him up while he robs the house. Then, with a sick heart, he realizes that Mr. Mitchell might not even live here anymore. For all he knows, Mr. Mitchell might be dead. Maybe it's too late. Maybe no matter what, it's too late. The thought makes him turn away, take a few steps back towards his car. He sneezes. The sudden fierce sneeze jerks his head up and down in the coldness of the night, seems to jar something loose in his mind. He wipes at his nose with the back of a cold bare hand, takes a breath, and walks up the steps to the front porch of the house.

His hands hang at his sides and he squeezes them open and shut. He's hyperventilating. This is crazy. As a little kid he'd stood at this door trick-or-treating on Halloween. Mr. Mitchell was a salty, friendly type. Paul has some faint memory of this door. The same yellowy light seems to be illuminating the front porch. He imagines it's even the same yellow bulb. What a great bulb to last all these years.

Stop it, he tells himself, stop thinking and do it. He rings the doorbell. He folds his hands under his armpits. Well, there you have it, Mr. Mitchell isn't home. Of course he isn't home. He doesn't live here anymore. He's dead. The futility makes him angry. He'll kick down the door and go in and steal the television. He'll go back to the bar; some of the guys there will know how to unload a T.V.

He hears a noise on the other side of the door and then he suspects that someone is eyeing him through the peephole. He makes a wave at the peephole, a lifting of the hand, the friend sign in old cowboy and Indian movies. He wouldn't open the door, he realizes. If he were looking out at himself, he wouldn't open the door. Snot runs from his nose. He's a monster. He's become a goddamn monster.

A lock releases, and then a spectacled man with thin gray hair looks out at him with the door still held by a chain lock. The face bears some resemblance to Mr. Mitchell. Some familiar essence of Mr. Mitchell swims out at him through the haze of years gone by. But it's not the lively, friendly face of the man who hopped up at his son's basketball games. This face looks worn, reserved, cautious, the look of a man who spends much time alone, maybe goes out for the lunch special at the new strip mall on the edge of town.

"Mr. Mitchell?"

The old man squints at him through the space allowed by the chain lock. "Yes?"

Paul takes his hands out from under his armpits. A breath passes through him like a wave. He feels a sudden surge of hope, almost a feeling of love toward Mr. Mitchell, and it occurs to him that he hasn't spoken to anyone he knows in this town, this town of his youth, for many years.

"Mr. Mitchell, I'm Paul Davis."

The old man squints harder. "Do I know you?"

"I used to live around here, Mr. Mitchell."

Mr. Mitchell rubs at the side of his head, as if the light massage might help him process this information. His hand rises toward the chain lock, but he doesn't open the door. "Okay," he says. "Did you want something?"

"I knew Ned."

"You knew Ned?"

"Yes sir. We weren't really close friends. But I liked him. I was sorry to hear about the car accident, about...I'm sorry about Ned, sir, I know what happened after senior year. I think my folks...I think my folks sent flowers. We all felt real bad."

Mr. Mitchell lets out a long breath and his shoulders slump. His hand rests more fully on the chain lock. Then he slides the chain off and opens the door wide. "Come in out of the cold." He steps back and Paul slinks in, head down, as if called into the principal's office. He stamps the snow from his shoes, realizes his feet are freezing. He doesn't have the proper footgear. He shuffles the soles of his shoes against the inner mat.

"Don't worry about that, son."

He sounds a little more like himself, like the gruffly friendly man Paul recalls. Mr. Mitchell shuts the door behind them and Paul lifts his eyes and sees that Mr. Mitchell is much smaller than he remembers

124

him, frail, almost weightless he seems, and shorter too. Paul could overpower him and tie him up in a flash if it came to that. Still, he trembles in front of Mr. Mitchell.

"Do you want coffee?" Mr. Mitchell asks.

"Oh no sir, thank you. I'm not...I'm just going to be here a minute."

Mr. Mitchell frowns at him. "Have you been drinking, son?"

"Some. I'm sorry. I'm not drunk."

"You'd better have some coffee. Sit down." He points Paul toward a couch with a coffee table in front of it.

"All right."

"Do you want cream and sugar?"

"No thanks. Well, cream. No sugar. You don't need to go to any trouble."

"It's already made. I've just got to microwave it. You mind old coffee?"

"No sir. I like old coffee."

Mr. Mitchell frowns at him. "You sit right there. Go on. Sit there."

"I will."

Mr. Mitchell frowns at him again to make sure he really is going to sit, and then he walks into the kitchen.

Paul sits as instructed and looks about the house which he has only been in once before, on the night he robbed it. He's not the sort of person who's observant about houses, decorations, that sort of thing, but he remembers with surprising clarity the layout of the house, the placement of the rooms off the hallway, where the bathrooms are and the master bedroom with the closet where they'd found the gun hidden on a shelf beneath some sweaters. The den where he's sitting has the feel of a room that hasn't been properly cleaned for a while. Not dirty really, but dusty, and there are magazines and newspapers strewn about on the coffee table and on assorted other end tables. The pictures on the wall seem like they were put up many years before and never changed.

Mr. Mitchell comes back into the room carrying a cup with no saucer and Paul clears a space on the coffee table in front of him. Mr. Mitchell sets the cup down, sighing and putting a hand to his back as he bends over.

He straightens up. "I'll get my own cup now," he says.

Paul nods. "Thanks very much. I didn't mean to trouble you."

"It's no trouble."

He goes back into the kitchen and Paul tastes his coffee. Old. He hates old coffee. And it has sugar in it as well as cream. He'll forget the whole thing. He'll make up some story and get the hell out of here.

Mr. Mitchell returns and sits down in an armchair across from Paul, using the same coffee table to hold his cup. He nods at Paul. "You knew Ned?"

"Yes sir."

"Why are you here?"

He swallows. This is going to be harder than he thought. He's not sure if he can talk.

Mr. Mitchell's eyebrows lift. He looks now like a tough old coot. Hadn't he been in the war? Paul seems to remember something about that now.

Mr. Mitchell leans forward. "Talk, son. What is it? What brings you here?"

"I...a long time ago, Mr. Mitchell...Ned...I did something wrong..."

Mr. Mitchell's eyes widen. "Is it something you and Ned did? If it was, I don't want to hear about it. Do you understand? I don't want to know now."

"No sir, Mr. Mitchell. No. It was nothing Ned did. I robbed a house. Me and a couple of other boys robbed a house. A long time ago. We were just kids."

His eyebrows lift. "Whose house?"

"Yours."

Mr. Mitchell rubs at the side of his head, in that massaging motion to clear his mind. "This house never got robbed."

"Yes it did. We robbed it. We came in behind that hedge on the side of your house."

The old man sips his coffee and nods slowly. "There is a hedge there all right. I trimmed it back a couple of years ago, but it grew back."

"It covers everything. You can't see anything, from the road."

"When was this, son? When did you rob my house? What year?"

"It was the same year Ned...It would have been our senior year."

The old man breathes. He stares across the coffee table at Paul. He sets his cup on the table and sinks back in his armchair, closing his eyes and rubbing at the side of his face. "I don't want to know anything more," he says. "I think you should go now." Then his eyes pop open. "Why are you telling me this? Why are you telling me this now?"

"I thought..."

"You thought it was time to tell me, and you'd feel better about it somehow."

Paul's throat tightens. He looks down. "I guess so."

"Feel better then," the old man says. "You told me about it and now you can feel better. You can go now."

"We stole..."

"I don't want to know what you stole, son."

"I'm sorry, sir. It was a bad thing to do."

The old man takes off his glasses and stares at Paul with empty, dead eyes, unblinking eyes that take him in with revulsion so that Paul's gut wrenches as if he's seeing himself through those eyes.

"I know what you stole. You stole a gun."

"Yes sir."

"You made it look like nobody had even been in."

He looks up at Mr. Mitchell. "You were at Ned's basketball game."

Now it's the old man who's struggling to talk. Paul hears the way his voice constricts, and he seems to speak more to himself now than to Paul. "When I realized that gun was missing, I blamed Ned. We were having some problems. Nothing we couldn't have worked out. I thought he'd taken that gun and sold it or done something wrong with it and we fought over that and one thing led to another and there were harsh words. He moved out to stay with his older sister. He got killed that summer and we'd never made it right."

"No," Paul whispers. He stares at Mr. Mitchell in horror. "God no," he says, using his voice to ward off something wild and dangerous. "No, that couldn't have been the only thing. You'd have fought over something..."

"Goddamn you." The old man sobs and lunges across the coffee table. Paul catches him in his arms and eases him onto the sofa cushions. The old man lies there for a moment, still as death, then springs at him again. He rips his fingernails across Paul's cheek and Paul pushes him away and bolts for the door. He runs down the front steps and Mr. Mitchell follows him and screams from the porch, "Who were those other boys? Who were they?"

He runs for his car. He struggles with the door, Mr. Mitchell's screams tearing at him.

He drives. He drives as fast as he can away from the house, careening through the snowy streets. A few blocks away a police cruiser's spinning lights fill the rear view mirror.

When the policeman walks up, he shines a flashlight through the open window, and Paul raises a hand to shield his tear-filled eyes from the glare.

In the Bar

I come into the bar about sundown. The boys whisper low when they see what I'm carrying. They move aside so I can belly up to the bar, but they glance sidelong at me. Things will heat up fast. Minnie, the bartender, keeps her back to me, rinsing a glass, eyeing me through the barroom mirror.

Old Cole is the first to work up his nerve. "What are you doing tonight, Doc?"

I slap Slim, my trusty pen, down on the bar top, along with a notebook. "Writing."

"Holy mother of pearl," he mutters. The boys gasp and slide farther away.

"That's right, by God, I'm writing tonight! Drinks on the house, Minnie!"

She turns slowly and smiles. "We don't want any trouble, Doc. Why don't you put that pen away before you do something you'll regret in the morning?"

I pick up Slim and aim it at her heart. "I'll put it away when I'm good and ready. But before I do, I mean to use it."

I look at the boys. They'd been hard on my last story. The criticism had been harsh and unrelenting. But they'd be sorry for that now.

I hear a laugh, a long, low, whoosh of air laugh. Lou. Laptop Lou. The harshest critic of them all and a hardass who's been embraced by the literary arts committee in our town.

He sits there with his computer, tapping away. He calls out the side of his mouth, "Looks like we got a throwback here, boys. A pen and paper man."

I point Slim at his head and he stops laughing. "I wouldn't aim that old ink thrower if you don't intend to use it," he says.

130

"I'll use it, all right."

He rocks back in his chair, typing with one finger. "Big talker."

I turn to Minnie. "Whiskey."

"Doc," she warns, "we all know what will happen if you drink even a single drop."

My pen swings back at her. She feels it, touching her down deep, in that place where even Laptop Lou with his golden metaphors has never touched her, touches her in that way that makes us both forget who we are and where we come from, makes us wake sometimes on a sand hill back of town wondering how we got there and not caring either, only knowing we have each other and the stars as we rise and brush the burrs from our shorts.

Her hand wavers on a shot glass.

"Not a shot, baby. Make it a tumbler."

Old Cole whistles low. "You know what will happen if he gets even a single drop."

"Pour it, Minnie," I say softly. "Pour it hard. Pour it fast. Pour it light and sweet."

She stares into my eyes. "Are you on tonight, Doc? Or are you faking it? Because I don't think I can get all worked up again and be let down if you can't use your pen."

My face twitches. One eyebrow hangs too low. I can't lie to her. "I never know anymore, Minnie. The hands..." I hold up the right. "This one's rickety. Sometimes it just freezes up. I overused it, I guess. But this one..." I hold up the left. "I used to switch off and on. I could swing both ways. But you know about the book I dropped on it three winters ago. I guess everybody around here knows about that."

"Damn fool," Laptop Lou says. "Damn fool could have used a computer program with a built-in dictionary. But hell no. Mr. Throwback picks up a Webster's. Heavy job. Drops it right on his knuckles.

Broke them into pieces." He laughs his whoosh job laugh.

I step toward him.

"Easy, Doc." Minnie reaches across the bar and holds my sleeve.

"Pour it, baby."

Could this be the night, once again, that we wind up on the sand hill south of town, half-blinded, burrs in our shorts, the stars burning with a miracle of brightness above our heads, the sand playing like a fine melancholy dust between our thighs? When that happens, we cry like babies.

She looks into my eyes and pours.

Old Cole shakes his head mournfully. "If he gets even a single drop, he'll bark like a dog."

Dead silence in the bar. Even Laptop Lou stops his infernal tapping on the keyboard. I hold the tumbler high, and now I give a toast to the ancient muses and pour the entire glass over my head. Whisky runs down my cheek. My tongue flicks out and captures one single drop. It explodes through my cranium with a white heat light. My back spasms. My teeth snap at the air. Minnie steps back against the gilded mirror and puts her hand to her mouth, and Old Cole slides away as I hop on one foot, trying to hold the sound in, but now it bursts out of me like some evil genie spewing forth. I tilt my chin to the chandeliers and bark like a dog.

"My God, I warned you all," Old Cole says.

I hop around the bar, pinching noses and ears and knuckling foreheads. I dance by Laptop Lou and it hits me, a sudden inspiration. It' my right hand he's watching, my good if rickety right, but it's my dead left that blind-sides him, sneaks in and hits the Don't Save button, and in a flash the Hell Yes I'm Sure button. It's gone. His text is gone. He stares in disbelief at the screen. He takes a breath, steadying himself. He taps

132

at some keys. Then he taps harder. He taps all over the place. Sweat breaks out on his forehead. He stares at the cold dead heartless screen. A wasteland. The abyss.

"You primitive piece of shit!" he shouts. "You screwed me out of a first draft!"

He bolts for the bar and before I can stop him, he rips pages from my notebook, shredding them, and as I try to pin his arms, he goes for Slim. He's got it up halfway and everybody's ducking for cover, but Minnie, my love, my brave love, is hanging in there with me, batting at his wrist with a fifth of tequila. The good stuff. Jose Cuervo.

"Grab it, Minnie," I tell her.

I know she's scared. She doesn't see many of them anymore. And Slim is a doozy, long and straight, more weight than you'd expect. Little gold tip at the end. It's loaded. If that bastard gets control of it, we're in for a rough time. He elbows me in the ribs, breaks my grip, and then I hear the whoosh of his side mouth laughter stop.

Minnie's holding Slim, aiming it right between his eyes.

"Get out, Lou," she says, "and take your filthy laptop with you."

"There was a time you didn't think it was so filthy." I can hear the tears in his voice. Pretty boys like him break quick.

"Yeah, so what? It was new back then. Every two bit poet and cowboy carries one now. There aren't many who carry what Doc has. Or knows how to use it the way he does."

He's got one final trick up his sleeve. He stuffs several of my pages into his mouth and chews.

"My God," Old Cole says, "that will be hell to decode."

I toss Laptop Lou into the street and Old Cole pitches his laptop on top of him. Lou picks up the computer and runs down the street. A howling wind rushes him along. He'll run to Momma. He'll ask Momma about that Don't Save button. I know him. He's my brother. But that's the subject of a different story.

Minnie watches me as I come back into the bar. "I'm sorry you lost some pages, honey."

"They were mostly blanks. A philosophical note or two. A grocery list. Some stuff about the end of the world." I look into her eyes. I speak softly now. "But you're still holding something."

She gasps, realizing she's still holding Slim.

"Easy." I reach out. "Just relax. Let me take it. Nice and slow, now."

She puts it in my hand, drops it in sweet and light, and then she steps back with a triumphant smile, sweat beading above her full, luscious, upper lip. She's done it. She's
handled Slim and come out alive and unwounded, and I close my hand around Slim and hold it for a moment before we both realize what I've done.

Her eyes widen. "You took it in your left hand," she says.

"I couldn't have," I whisper.

"No way," Old Cole says. "No way a man can grip a pen like that when his hand's been busted up by a Webster's."

Minnie slowly pushes my notebook toward me, finding a fresh page behind all the ripped and torn pages.

I make a mark on the page, one single solitary stroke, a crummy feeble little mark really, and she stares down at it in dismay. Old Cole looks over my shoulder. "Looks like a lazy Q," he offers.

I frown. "Could be a Z."

Minnie's lip quivers. "I don't think it's a letter at all."

"Sure it is," I say, but the awful truth is battering at me. My whole head hums. Maybe the left is dead after all. Maybe it's madness to think you can ever be as good again.

"Try the right then," Old Cole suggests.

I start to make the switch, but then it's all clear before my eyes. Give up one hand and what do you have left? Just another hand and then you use that one up, too, and pretty soon you're out of hands, and someone like Laptop Lou will be there whispering: throwback, throwback, throwback. No, I wasn't going out that way. If I was going out, it was going to be now, with the left.

"Whiskey," I say.

She pushes the tumbler toward me. I keep Slim in my left hand. I'm not dropping Slim now, not after what we've been through together. I pick the tumbler up with my right hand and pour it over my head. My tongue darts out like a frog after a fly and I swallow a single drop. My back arches up like a cat stretching. My shirt rips across the back. I hope up on the bar and steam foot up and down. I babble, speaking in tongues, and then my chin tilts up toward the ceiling and I bark like a dog.

"I'm writing, boys!"

"God help us all," Old Cole mutters.

Slim hooks out, slashes a big V across the barroom mirror. I swing from the chandeliers, raking couplets on the ceiling, and as the boys try to drag me down, I leap off, running around the bar, covering the wallpaper with witty epitaphs and aphorisms and a quickly written soliloquy about death and dying.

"Give him paper!" Minnie cries.

The boys get me in a headlock, drag me to the bar, and shove paper in front of me.

135

And I go, oh yeah, Doc is back, boys, Doc is back, and Old Cole is beside me now, feeding the paper to me as fast as he can. They're sending out for more. I've gone through five reams, we're down to cardboard and paper sacks when Laptop Lou steps back into the bar and shouts wickedly, "Jesus saves!"

I whirl. I take aim, but my hand freezes up.

"Momma saved my draft!" Laptop Lou cries. He holds up his laptop and he taps away, steady and low, sure of himself, clickety, clickety, click, and Minnie shrinks back against the barroom mirror and I know it's too late. Slim falls out of my hand to the bar. My left lies withered and broken on the bar top beside it, and I know, deep down in my gut, that you never come back from a bout with a Webster's.

My shoulders slump. I'm a throwback. Laptop Lou is the future.

Laptop Lou taps out his love note to Minnie. Sorry, I mouth to her, we'll always have the sand hill.

But before I can stop her, she picks up Slim, and with her other hand she pours a tumbler of whiskey.

She looks into my eyes, then raises her glass over her head and pours. One single drop finds its way to her flicking red tongue, and only an omniscient narrator would know what happens inside of her, but she tilts her chin to the ceiling and barks like a dog.

I could tell you the rest. I could tell you the way Laptop Lou stood there flatfooted, tapping away until finally he just kept hitting the File key, until Old Cole mercifully pried the laptop from his cold fingers. Or I could tell you the way I called out the words to Minnie as she burned up the pages, until finally I didn't need to tell her anything at all. She simply knew, as if she had dreamed it in the way I used to once, every letter, every word, every sentence, every story coming to her as if she'd known them all along. I could tell you all that and how I later sought therapy for the left, how, as it turns out, there are support groups for those damaged by a Webster's. But I don't really want to tell you any of that. What I want to tell you is the truest thing I know, which is that Minnie and I woke up on the sand hill south of town, half-blinded, moist with love, the stars burning overhead, the sand playing like a fine melancholy dust between our thighs. We cried like babies.

About the Author

Robert Garner McBrearty was awarded the 2007 Sherwood Anderson Foundation Fiction Award for stories included in this collection. His other writing awards include a Pushcart Prize and fellowships to the Macdowell Colony and the Fine Arts Work Center in Provincetown, MA. His short stories have appeared in North American Review, Narrative, StoryQuarterly, Missouri Review, New England Review, Mississippi Review, Green Hills Literary Lantern, and many other places. As well, his stories have been frequently used for large dramatized readings at Stories on Stage in Denver and at the Dallas Museum of Art. He is the author of a previous collection of stories, *A Night at the Y*. Currently, he teaches writing at the University of Colorado in Boulder, and also serves as an Assistant Editor for Narrative magazine.